FIRST DOWN

A SISTER'S BEST FRIEND ROMANCE

ELLA KADE

FIRST DOWN

Join Ella's mailing list to be the first to know of new releases, free books, sales, and other giveaways!

https://ellakade.com/newsletter/

My twin sister's best friend is off-limits...

But that hasn't stopped me from loving her for the past five years.

Every chance my sister gets, she reminds me and Lo of my manwhore ways. That was long before I ever knew she existed, and now I only have eyes for her—but I'm keeping my hands to myself.

After her horrific sexual assault, Lo sleeps in my bed, lives in my house, and invades my every thought.

Now that she's away from my sister whispering in her ear,

warning her away, she's too fragile for me to think about starting something that may wreck us both.

She's not ready for me, and the longer she's here, the more my past mistakes come back to haunt me, making me realize I might never deserve her.

ONE
OZ

JULY

BEER BOTTLES and pizza boxes littered the living room floor. Ford and Fin argued about what gun was best as they played in a Call of Duty's War Zone tournament. Neither could agree, and I didn't care, so I zoned out, thinking about how difficult football practice was going to be when it started in a couple of days. I'd been slacking for the last month on working out, and I was going to pay for it.

Tonight was my first night in the new house Fin had bought at the beginning of summer. It wasn't much, but it got us out of the football house and into our own place where no one could bother us. I would have been here sooner, but I stayed back in Santa Lucia an extra couple of days so that I could help Dani and Lo move back to UCLA. I then spent the next week dealing with my blackmailer, Dean.

Fin, my best friend since first grade, sat down beside me and clapped his hand on my shoulder. His black hair had grown out a little more over the summer. The sides were shaved, and the length hung over his forehead and covered one eye.

"How'd the move with the girls go?" He asked, watching as Ford tried to teach West how to play the game they were playing.

"Besides them having a lot of shit? Fine, but next time I'm not doing it alone. You're helping."

"I'm an asshole, but my boyfriend was finally coming home, and I wanted to spend some time alone with him before all you assholes moved in," Fin grumbled.

"Well, I could have moved in a couple of weeks ago, and then you wouldn't have gotten your alone time." I flashed him a smile, knowing he wouldn't like my smart-ass remark.

Fin shoved my shoulder and let out a grumbled 'asshole' before he flashed his own smile at me, letting me know he was going to say some asshole remark. "I would have kicked you out and made you sleep in the yard."

He probably would have.

"Did you at least make any headway with Lo? Ask her on

a date while you were in the same town as her for the summer?"

I kept my gaze on the TV, ignoring him. He knew the answer to his question and only wanted to give me shit. I'd been in love with Lo since our freshman year in high school when she moved to my hometown and became best friends with my twin sister, Danica.

The only thing was Lo's off-limits.

I was a bit of a manwhore before Lo came into my life. I got an early start, and by the time we started high school, I'd gone through most of the female population in our small town that was my age and had a bad reputation with the ladies. Since Lo became the object of my desire, I haven't been with many women, but a guy has needs, and five years was a long ass time to wait.

Dani seemed to love to remind me of my manwhore ways when Lo was in the room, which made it seem pointless even to try making her see me in a different light. Who knew what my sister said to her when I wasn't around? And it wasn't even like Dani and I didn't get along. We did. She was my best friend next to Fin.

My phone rang, lighting up with Dani's picture on it. Speak of the devil.

"Hey, miss me already?"

"Oz?" Dani cried.

I sat up ramrod straight, hearing how upset she was.

"What's wrong?"

At hearing my tone, Fin sat forward and turned to look at me, mouthing. 'what's going on?'.

I lifted the shoulder that wasn't attached to my phone.

"It's Lo," she sobbed.

Jumping up, I started to pace the small living room floor. "What about her?"

"Oz, it's bad. Really bad. I can't... even... can you come here? We need you."

"I'm on my way," I said as I patted down the pockets of my cargo shorts, checking for my keys. When I felt them, I headed for the front door.

A heavy hand stopped me on my shoulder. "What the fuck, man? Are you headed to LA?"

"Yeah, something's happened with Lo, and Dani asked me to come. I've got to go." I shrugged his hand off my shoulder and pulled out my keys.

I heard him jog down the stairs as he shouted. "Do you need me to come?"

Beeping the locks on my car, I looked at him. "I don't know. I haven't heard Dani sound like that since Pookie died."

"And she wouldn't tell you why?" He turned to look back at the house and then at me.

"No, but they need me, so I'm going. It's okay. You can stay. It will be a long drive." I opened my car door.

"No, I'm coming. Just give me a second."

"One second," I called back. There was no way I could wait any longer than that.

I'd hit the engine start button when Fin and West came barreling down the stairs. Fin got into the passenger seat, and West slid in the back behind his boyfriend.

We said nothing on the normally three-hour drive that took a little more than two hours. My mind raced with the possibilities of what could have happened that would have led Dani to call me crying. She was a tough chick, and I knew deep down in my soul it was bad.

I parked what seemed like a football field away from the entrance to their dorm and sprinted to the door, not thinking about how I wouldn't be able to get in. Luckily, Fin was on it and texted Dani to come down and meet us. At least someone had their head about them. The last two hours had been the longest of my life.

Dani showed up downstairs, and with one look at my sister, I knew nothing I had imagined could compare to what really happened to Lo. Dani's face was streaked with tears, her eyes were puffy and red-rimmed, and she looked like she was about to drop from exhaustion.

Did Lo have cancer?

We followed Dani as she dragged her body up three flights of stairs. I wrapped my arm around her waist and let her lean on me for support. She was dead on her feet, and that was a lot coming from an athlete.

Stopping outside their room door, Dani looked at me with pleading eyes filled with tears.

"Before you go in, you should know. I don't know how she's going to react, but you were the only person I could think to call. She didn't want me to call her parents or her brother, so…"

"Just tell us already," Fin softly demanded, which was an improvement for him. "What happened to Lo?"

Tears started streaming down Dani's face. "She was raped."

TWO
OZ

JULY

MY WORLD WAS RIPPED out from under me, and I would have fallen if it weren't for Fin and West there to catch me.

"I had to have heard you wrong?" Fin growled out, sounding from a distance. I felt like I was being plunged underwater and drowning with each breath I attempted.

"It happened on her way home. She went to grab us something to eat while I was in the shower and..." Dani collapsed against my already wobbly frame. I needed to pull myself together for both of them, but mainly for Lo. She couldn't see how badly this was affecting me when she was going through something no one should ever go through.

Wrapping my arms around my sister, I kissed her forehead. "This happened when?"

"A little over a week ago." She turned her face into my chest and let out a torrent of tears, soaking my shirt.

"Why the hell did you wait so long to call me?" My frustration slipped through.

"She wouldn't let me until today. She's barely left the bedroom, and when she does, it's only to go to the bathroom like twice a day. She's withering away, and I knew something needed to change."

"Has she gone to the police? The hospital?" I asked in rapid-fire succession.

"She won't go. She's afraid to leave the room. She's afraid that the evil asshole who did this to her will find her again."

"Was she a virgin?" Fin blurted out, making me want to kill him.

West clapped his hand over Fin's mouth and narrowed his eyes at him. "Ignore him. He's worried, and it came out wrong."

"Of course, I care about her." It came out all muffled from behind West's hand.

"What can we do?" West asked softly.

Pulling out of my arms, Dani unlocked their dorm suite door and held the door open. At first, all I saw were tissues littering the floor, but then I heard it—Lo's keening in the background. She sounded like a wounded animal.

Dani hung her head as she wiped her eyes. "She said she doesn't want to be here anymore, but she wouldn't leave with me. I can't protect her."

"But we can," I answered.

"I think so," Dani nodded. "Go and try to talk to her, Oz."

I wasn't sure what I could do if she wouldn't listen to Dani, but I'd try. I'd do anything for Lo—even give up my own life for her to never feel this pain.

"You guys hang out here." I motioned to the hard-as-a-rock couch the school had provided.

"We'll be here if you need us," West said before dragging Fin over to the couch with him.

Fin looked like he was close to murder as he stared in the direction of Lo's room. His jaw ticked, and his hands clenched at his sides. He was the mirror image of me. I knew I needed to calm down before I went inside. Being ready to murder anyone and anything that came within a mile's radius of her wouldn't do Lo any good.

I tapped on the door to alert her I was coming in so I wouldn't freak her out.

Cracking the door open, I peeked my head inside. "Lo," I called quietly. "It's me, Oz. Can I come in?"

She made a noise. I wasn't sure if Lo wanted me to be here

or not, but I couldn't hold back any longer from seeing her. I closed the door and slowly made my way over to her bed. Lo was facing me with the covers pulled up to her chin, and her body was curled up in the fetal position. Normally I would have sat on the side of the bed, but I wasn't sure how she felt about having anyone from the male persuasion that close to her, so I sat on the floor with my back against the wall on the opposite side of Dani's bed and tried to take her in. The room was barely lit by the streetlight outside, making it difficult to see her.

Unsure what to say, I stayed quiet for what felt like hours but was probably only twenty or thirty minutes before I spoke. "Can I come sit by you if I stay on the floor?"

She let out a shaky yes that had my insides raging to murder whoever did this to her. Why would anyone want to hurt her beautiful soul?

I crawled over on my hands and knees, letting her see my movement, and then sat so I was close but I wasn't in her face. I placed my hand on the bed and left it there, letting Lo decide if she wanted to take it. If it were up to me, Lo would never have to do another thing she didn't want to do in her life.

After a few minutes, one of her fingers reached out and touched mine. There's my girl.

"I don't think I'm ever going to be able to get out of this bed," she cried softly.

Resting my forehead on the edge of her mattress so she couldn't see how devastated I was for her, I hooked my finger with hers. "I can't even begin to fathom what you're going through right now, but I can promise you I will never let another human being hurt you again until I take my last dying breath. Even then, I'll still protect you. Nothing like this will ever happen to you again."

"How are you going to do that?" She asked, her voice barely above a whisper.

"I'll stay by your side and be your bodyguard." Even as I said the words, I knew I would. I would also look into getting her a dog that would protect her, one loyal only to her.

She pulled on my hair, giving it a tug. "How are you going to do that when you live three hours away?"

Lifting my head, I locked my eyes with hers. I wanted her to know I was serious. I hoped she could see it and, if not, hear it in my voice. "I'll drop out of school and move here. Whatever you need."

She gave a slight shake of her head. "You can't do that. I won't let what happened to me ruin two lives."

"I'd do it for you."

She pulled her hands up under her chin, retreating. "I know you would. That's the kind of guy you are, but I can't ask you to do that. I don't know what to do. I can't go home.

My parents will say they told me not to live in LA. Like nothing bad happens anywhere else in the world."

Bad things happened everywhere, but I wasn't going to say that.

"I doubt they'd say that. They love you." If her parents even thought those words, I'd crush them.

"I don't want to be here, but I don't know where to go to feel safe," she said on a shaky breath. "Do I join a convent?"

It was then that I knew what I had to do, and before I could think about it, the words were slipping from my lips. "Come home with me. You can stay there as long as you need."

There was a long pause before she spoke. "I… I don't know about that."

"Why not? You'll have four big football players there to protect you, and maybe we can talk Fin into getting a dog."

"You'd try to convince Fin to let me have a dog?" Her face scrunched up, and she let out a sob.

"I'd do anything for you, Lo. All you need to do is ask." I wanted so badly to comfort her, but knew my touch wouldn't likely be wanted. "Come stay with us. School doesn't start for another few weeks, so you won't be missing anything. I have football practice, but I can talk to Coach and see if I can get out of it."

She tilted her head, keeping her eyes closed, but it seemed like she wanted to be closer to me. "I seriously doubt your coach is going to let you miss out on practice while I'm there."

"So, you're coming?" I asked, a little too upbeat. I shouldn't be this happy to get her into my house after what she's been through.

Her eyes opened and locked on mine. "Do you think Dani will be mad if I leave?"

"She's your best friend and wants what's best for you. So if coming to Willow Bay will help, then she'd want you to go."

"This has been the longest week of my life. It hasn't even been a week, I don't think, and yet it feels like it's been at least a year. I can't stop watching the door, thinking he's going to find me. What if he finds me and kills me?" Her words got higher with each word each spoke.

"I'm not going to let that happen." I cleared my throat and asked what I knew had to be asked. "Did you know him?"

Curling deeper into herself, she answered with a broken voice. "No, but I'd seen him around last semester. He always seemed like a creeper at parties, but I have no idea what his name is."

Had this asshole rapist targeted Lo?

"Dani said you haven't been to the hospital or the police station." I tried to spur her on to explain why she hadn't yet.

When she only stared at me in the dark, I had to question why.

"I can't. You don't know what it feels like. There's no way I can tell some stranger what happened on the worst day of my life. They'll want to invade me further and, I just…" Turning her face into her pillow, Lo broke, sobbing until her body was heaving.

"No, I can't understand. No matter how much I want to, but I will abide by your wishes. Do you want Dani to come in here and pack a bag for you or—"

"Can you tell her I'm going to leave for a little while and stay with you?" She stuttered out between sobs.

"I can. Just a heads up, Fin and West came with me. They were—no, they are worried about you. Do you want me to stay out there with them or…"?

"Stay out there. It won't take me long. I just want to get out of here as quickly as possible." She covered her face with her hands and cried.

I hovered my hand over her head, wanting to help ease some of her pain, but knew it could have the exact opposite effect. Instead, I left the room to find Dani, Fin, and West sitting on the edge of their seats, looking at me with hopeful eyes the second I walked out.

Jumping up, Dani ran to me. Holding her in my arms, I hugged her tight. "Did she talk to you?"

"Some. I didn't get much, only that she doesn't want to

report it, and," I looked over to where Fin and West were sitting. "She's going to come home with us to stay."

West, of course, reacted exactly as I was expecting with acceptance of what I'd just told them, but Fin looked at the wall like he could see through it. "We've only got three bedrooms. Where's she going to sleep?"

"I'm going to give her my room. I can sleep out on the couch until she decides to come back here." Resting my chin on Dani's head, I hugged her tighter, thinking about how this could have easily happened to her. "I know she said she doesn't want to report it, but can you see if she has any bruises or anything? We had the light off the entire time, and I couldn't see much."

Pulling back to look up at me, Dani's eyes filled with tears. "You need to be prepared, Oz. She's beaten up pretty bad even as the bruises have started to fade. Her face is all swollen and bruised."

"You need to take pictures in case she changes her mind. Anywhere there's evidence," I gritted out, hating the thought of Lo having to go through the shame of having her abuse photographed.

Fin stood and started to pace around the small living space. "What're photos going to do if she doesn't know who it is?"

"She said she knows who he is. Not his name, but she's

seen him around campus. I'm confident she'd be able to pick him out of a picture or a lineup."

"Did this asshole target her?" Fin gritted out.

"That's my thought. Maybe he saw her back after break and assaulted her since she was alone."

"Oh, God. I should have gone with her. How am I ever going to forgive myself?" Dani cried.

Looking down at my sister, I spoke quietly in case Lo could hear us. "You need to pull yourself together, so you can go in there and be strong for her. Lo wants your help packing a bag, and before she leaves with us, you need to try and get the pictures."

Dani shook her head. "I don't think that's going to go over well."

"Probably not, but tell her you'll download them to your computer and lock them up so no one will see them, but that she needs to do it in case she ever needs the evidence." I wasn't sure Lo would be convinced, but we had to try before it was too late.

Dani's eyes filled with tears as she looked toward the bedroom. "I still can't believe someone attacked her on the way from her car to the dorm."

I couldn't either. "I think that's why she doesn't feel safe, and the fact that she kind of knows the guy."

"I'm going to call my coach tomorrow and see if he'll let

me out of practice for a week or so, and if he does, I'll come and stay with her there. If that's okay?" Dani asked.

"Sounds good, but don't get in trouble over it. Lo will have the four of us watching out for her, and the only time I'll leave her alone is when I'm at practice." My gaze shifted toward Fin, and I grimaced. "I told her I'd try to convince you to get a dog to be with her when we're gone."

"Fucking hell, man. Why'd you have to go and do that? You know I can't say no now," he grimaced.

The first grin since Dani called me spread across my face. "Good, it will make her feel better."

"She's going to have to potty-train it. There's no way in hell I'm cleaning up dog piss or shit that's on my floor," Fin grumbled.

West slung his arm around Fin's shoulders and kissed his cheek. "He really is a softie deep down inside."

Dani motioned to the front of the bedroom door. "Does that," she tilted her head toward Fin and West. "Ever get weird?"

I shrugged. It didn't bother me. It was nice to see Fin happy for once in his life, and if he was happy with West, then I was all for it. "Not really. They're not overly affectionate in front of others, but when they are, I don't mind."

"I still can't believe Fin likes guys," she whispered.

"I don't think Fin likes guys," I stated quietly. "He likes

West, and that's all that matters. He's a much happier person now with West by his side and his parents out of his life."

"Can you imagine if our dad treated us like his dad did him?" Her eyes widened. "I can't believe he tried to make it so that Fin couldn't get a job anywhere in California."

"Yeah, well, he got what was coming to him for trying to fuck Fin over. Everyone in Santa Lucia hates him now. I wouldn't be surprised if they move away by the end of the year."

"If Fin's happy, then I'm happy," she nodded.

"Good, now I know you don't want to do what you have to do, but we need to be strong for Lo," I placed my hand on her shoulder. "If you need me to come in, just call, and I'll be right there."

"Thanks, big bro." She hugged me once more before she opened the bedroom door and slipped inside. I could only hear a few muffled words before I went back into the living area and sat down with Fin and West.

"You know if we keep adding people to the house, we're going to have to finish the basement," West said, looking at a still pacing Fin.

Fin stopped and narrowed his eyes at us. "No one else is moving in. With Ford and Lo, we're going to have a full house. Hell, we don't even have a bed for everyone now."

"I don't need a bed. The couch will be fine," I tried to placate him.

"Will it be fine when someone wants to watch a movie or have people over and you want to go to sleep and they're sitting on your bed?"

"Alright, I see your point, but what else was I going to do. Lo's afraid if she leaves her room, her attacker is going to find her. No one is going to fuck with her at our house."

"They better not, or I'll fucking kill them," Fin growled out.

"It's nice to know you care," came Lo's soft voice from the hallway.

"I wouldn't be here if I didn't. Fuck, I'm sorry, Lo. If there's anything I can do, just let me know." He stopped pacing and looked out the window as if he didn't just do something totally out of the norm for him.

"You know what? You just did. Thanks, Fin. And you too, West. Thank you for coming when you had no idea what was going on and for letting me stay at your house. I promise to stay out of your way. I just can't stay here." By the time she's done speaking, Lo was full-on crying again.

"Oh hell, you don't need to thank us. You're part of the family now, and no one fucks with our family. You hear me?" Fin stepped toward Lo like he was going to hug her but then thought better of it.

Fin really had come a long way if he was counting Lo as family. He knew how much she meant to me, but still, he didn't have to bring her into his fold.

West stood and smiled softly at Lo. "Are you all packed?"

"Yeah, I… where did you park?"

"Hand me your keys, and I'll pull your car around to the door," Fin demanded.

I was glad he offered because I wasn't sure she could handle walking that far through the parking lot after finding out it had happened on her walk here.

Lo quietly thanked Fin as he walked out the door. He gave her a chin nod, with West following close behind.

Pausing at the door, West looked back and forth between us. "Do you need anything from us?"

"You're doing it, man. We'll be done in a few. Thanks," I gave him a thin smile.

The second the door closed, Dani and Lo both started crying. Dani paused with her arms out, and Lo fell into them, sobbing into her shoulder as if she'd never see her best friend again.

I tried to make the situation better by saying, "Hey, you can come back anytime you want, and Dani can visit anytime she wants. Plus, you can both talk on the phone."

"I know," Dani cried, hugging Lo tighter for a second and then letting her go. "If you need anything, day or night, you call me. I'm *always* here for you."

Lo nodded. "I will. I just need some time away from here and go to a place where I'll feel safe."

"I love you, Lo," Dani cried, handing me the suitcase she'd packed in the short time she'd been in the bedroom.

"Is this it?" I joked. The damn thing weighed close to fifty pounds.

"Shut up," Dani slapped my arm. "Give me a hug," she demanded.

I hugged her long and hard. "Don't be a stranger, sis, and be careful out there."

Instead of going down the stairs—I was afraid Lo might topple over from how weak she looked—we took the elevator down to the front entrance where Fin and West were waiting for us.

I helped Lo into the backseat of the car before I threw her suitcase in the trunk and took the other side of the backseat. I wished I had a blanket or something to wrap around her. She looked so cold over there as she leaned against the window, staring out the window with tears streaming down her cheeks and fogging up the window.

Not a single one of us spoke the entire way back to Willow Bay.

THREE
OZ

AUGUST

THE SOUND of Lo screaming had me flying up off the couch and running into my bedroom. She was flailing about, her legs fighting with the bedcovers as she tossed and turned to fight off her attacker. It had been the same for the last week. Every night, Lo cried out in her sleep, and every night, I went to her, trying to let her know she was safe.

Crawling in on the other side of the bed, I unwrapped the sheet from her legs and drew the covers up her body. Then I pulled her into my arms and let her cry into my chest until she fell back asleep. Every night Lo ended up falling asleep with her tiny body nestled against mine, and every morning she'd push away, unable to look at me.

I knew it was wrong to relish the nights she slept in my arms, but I couldn't help it. It was a dream of mine to have Lo in my bed. Just not like this. Never like this.

"I'm sorry," she cried, tightening her hold on me.

"You have nothing to be sorry about. It's perfectly natural for you to have nightmares," I told her in my most soothing voice.

"Still, you're barely sleeping, and you have practice. I've seen how difficult it is for you to drag yourself out of bed each morning."

She wasn't wrong, but was that the reason why she couldn't look at me each morning? Or was it because we'd slept with our bodies intertwined for hours on end, and she never had a nightmare when she was in my arms?

"I don't mind. Really, I don't. I'd happily get no sleep at all if it helps you get a night of peaceful sleep." I would give up everything for Lo to be the happy, carefree girl she was before that asshole took away the innocent way she once saw the world.

"I feel bad you're sleeping on the couch—or trying to. It can't be comfortable for a guy as big as you," she spoke into the darkness.

It wasn't comfortable. The only way to get any real sleep on that thing was if you drank until you passed out, but that wasn't happening now that football practice had started. Even though we didn't live in the football house, Coach did send someone to check on us each and every night.

I swear he probably gave all the places that sold alcohol pictures of everyone on the football team so they wouldn't sell to us. I'd heard a few of the guys complaining about not being able to buy any beer in all of Willow Bay. Coach was definitely putting in the extra effort to make sure we performed and would do our best to reach the Championship once again this year.

"See, you can't even deny it, can you?" she let out a humorous laugh, pulling away slightly.

"I can't deny the couch isn't comfortable, but it's fine. I'd sleep on a bed of nails if it were my only option." Internally, I groaned at sounding like a lovesick puppy.

Lifting her head to look up at me, she whispered as if anyone else in the house might overhear, "Am I waking up the other guys?"

"Not that I know of. If you have, they haven't mentioned it to me." And they probably wouldn't. No one was going to complain about Lo waking us up with her nightmares.

Wanting to break the tension from talk of nightmares, I turned on my side to face her better now that Lo wasn't against me. "Are you excited about going to pick out a puppy tomorrow?"

She nodded, and a small smile broke out on her pale face.

Her usually tanned complexion was washed out, and now Lo looked like she'd seen a ghost instead. It was like the color had been bleached from her body when he took what didn't belong to him.

"I'm really surprised Fin agreed. Although he did run through a list of rules for the puppy." She dipped her head. "It's obvious he's never owned a dog if he thinks a puppy is magically going to know not to go into his room or chew on his shoes." She let out a slight giggle, and it was music to my ears.

"He's never had a dog, but when I was growing up, we had a dog named Pookie, and it would chew up Fin's shoes while they were still on his feet." I scrunched up my face, thinking about it. "He wasn't a fan, and neither was Pookie."

"Then that makes it even more special he's letting me get one." She bowed her head. "And I did know about Pookie. Dani's shown me pictures. He was cute."

"He was, but he wasn't around for long. He got out one day and was hit by a car. After that, Dani swore she'd never have another dog again." How would Dani feel when Lo eventually went back to LA with a dog in tow?

"I can't imagine how awful that was for the both of you." She reached out her hand, and one finger touched my arm before she pulled back.

It blew my mind that Lo could sympathize with me after

what she went through, but that was the kind and amazing person she was.

"Thank you for letting me stay here. I'm not sure if I ever would have left my room if I was still back at UCLA. I kept feeling like he was constantly outside, looking up at my window. Do you think Dani would hate me if I never went back to LA?"

Leaning up on my elbow, I shook my head but knew she couldn't see me. "There's no way she'll ever hate you. Will Dani miss you if you decide to go to school somewhere else? Yes, but if you don't move halfway across the country, then she can come visit you."

"And what if I thought I wanted to go to school here?" Lo's voice was so quiet, I could barely hear her, and she was right next to me.

I, for one, would be very excited if Lo decided to go to Willow Bay University.

"I think Dani knows you're in good hands here and wouldn't be worried. It would give her more incentive to visit me with you here."

Curling back into herself, she peeked up at me. "We should have visited you more often instead of making you come to see us."

"That's okay. I know she was busy. I had football and school, and then she had soccer and school. If Dani wants to be in the Olympics one day, she needs to focus."

"You're a good brother. I wish I was as close to my family as you are to yours."

Even after all this time, I didn't know the dynamic with Lo's family. She spent most of her time at our house and hanging out with Dani. Lo went on vacations with us and everything like she was a part of the family, but she rarely talked about her own.

"I wish that too, but you'll always have us. You should probably try to get some sleep." It pained me to ask, but I did it anyway. "Do you want me to leave?"

She shook her head but didn't say anything. Instead, she pulled the covers up higher and then turned so that she was facing the other way. I wanted to hold her like I'd been doing earlier, but I followed her lead and turned the other way. She didn't need to wake up with my morning wood shoved against her back.

MY ALARM WAS GOING off in the other room, and I was lucky I could hear it. If this kept happening, I was going to need to set an alarm in my room. Each day, I woke up a little more exhausted than the day before, and if I overslept, Coach would have my hide.

"Is it morning already?" Lo moaned from the other side of the bed.

"Unfortunately, but you can go back to sleep. I'll just grab my clothes and hit the shower before I leave. I'll be home right after practice, but if you need anything, call or text me."

Lo rolled over, keeping her eyes closed. "Thank you again for last night."

"You don't have to thank me."

I grabbed my gym bag and a set of clothes before I headed into the bathroom. I needed the shower plus a gallon of coffee that I couldn't drink before practice to wake me up.

I didn't wait for the water to get warm. Stepping inside, I let the cold water jolt me awake before I slathered my hands with shower gel and ran them over my body. When my hand came into contact with my cock, I gave it a rough squeeze, hoping that would be enough, but it wasn't. My dick knew who'd been only feet away all night, and he didn't care if it was inappropriate or not to be hard over Lo. My head warred with my heart, but in the end, my dick won out.

My hand felt good. Too good. I hadn't seen any action in months. Not since the last time I got desperate enough to give up on the dream of Lo and me and fucked a random girl who was around. It was the second biggest mistake of my life and taught me to pick my randos more carefully. Meaning they couldn't be random, which meant that I needed to be in some type of relationship with her, which was also not going to happen.

Stroking my shaft in long, measured strokes, I pictured Lo at the beach in one of her teeny tiny bikinis that always drove me wild. It was always her I thought of when I got off, and now was no different. I imagined running up behind her and picking her up as I took us deeper into the water and running my cock along her ass. My hands splayed out on her stomach and dived into her bikini bottoms.

And then nothing. I couldn't. Even in my fantasy, I couldn't touch her anymore like I used to. It felt wrong knowing Lo wouldn't want me to touch her.

Closing my eyes, I beat myself off like I was trying to win a medal for the fastest jerk-off session in the history of all mankind. It wasn't fulfilling, but I guess it shouldn't be. Not like that.

Pissed off at myself, I hastily dried off and threw my clothes on before leaving the bathroom. Fin, West, and Ford were each standing in the kitchen with a protein shake in their hands. Fin nodded to the one sitting on the counter for me.

"Let's go, or we're going to be late," Fin grumbled. He so wasn't a morning person.

I followed behind the guys with our bags in tow. I set the alarm and then locked up the house. We were all quiet on the way to practice.

West turned in his seat to look back at me. "So, you're going to pick out a dog today?"

"That's the plan." I only hoped it was a good one.

"I think it will be good for her," Ford interjected like he was reading my thoughts. "It will give her something to take care of instead of thinking about what happened. Is she still having nightmares?"

"Every night," I sighed, wondering if I was helping her or not. "I'm surprised she doesn't wake you up."

"I sleep with fucking earplugs in, so I don't hear these two going at it," Ford jerked his thumb to the front where Fin and West were laughing at him.

"Your room is on the other side of the house, so it would be hard for us to hear her," West said, smiling. "Is she getting better?"

I shrugged because how the hell did I really know. "Maybe. I don't know. Last night instead of crying until she fell back to sleep, we talked a little. She said she doesn't want to go back to UCLA and was thinking of staying here to go to school."

"I'm sure you were on board with that plan," Fin said, looking back at me through the rear-view mirror. I couldn't see anything but his black eyes, but they were smiling.

"Of course, I want her here, but not for those reasons." Resting my head on the window, I looked out at nothing. "Now, nothing is ever going to happen between us. It can't."

"Why?" West asked, his voice curious.

"Because she was raped, and I can't imagine her wanting

any man to ever touch her again. I'll be the best friend I can for her, and that will have to be enough."

"I hate to say this, but it's true that many women who are sexually assaulted go on to be in healthy relationships," Ford stated matter of factly. "They have sex, and have children and… I don't know what else. But while it might seem like the end of the world for her right now, and she doesn't trust men to touch her with a ten-foot pole, Lo will return to normal. It might not be the same normal as before, but she won't always be the scared mouse she is right now."

Everyone turned to look at Ford. Where the hell had that come from?

No one said a word as we all stared at him for a moment, then Ford broke the silence. "You should talk to her about seeing a therapist. I think it would help."

"Who the hell are you?" Fin asked with an amused laugh.

"I know things." Ford turned to me. "All I'm saying is don't give up on her. I know it seems hopeless right now, but since the day I met you last year, I've known you were in love with her. Don't give up. Just give her time."

"I'll give her all the time she needs, but it doesn't help when Dani is always reminding her of me being with all the girls in our grade before Lo moved to Santa Lucia. Can't she see I've changed?" Slamming my head against the headrest, I close my eyes. "I barely fuck anyone anymore."

"Well, I suggest you fuck no one if you want a

relationship with her. Make them both see you've reformed, and all you want is Lo," West gave his wisdom from the front seat.

"Everyone is making too much sense today. Is it because I've barely slept since Lo moved in?" I grumbled.

"You're too close to the situation, and it's hard to see it clearly. The next time I see Dani, I'll tell her what a good boy you've been. It hasn't gone unnoticed that you haven't been with anyone since you've been here."

There was a reason for that, and even Fin didn't know it. I'd been trying very hard to keep my secrets from Santa Lucia from spilling into my life here in Willow Bay or for word getting back to Dani and Lo. But just when I thought it was over, either Dean or Tori would pop back into my life demanding more.

FOUR
LO

AUGUST

TURNING OFF THE CAR, Oz unclipped his seatbelt and turned to me. "Do you want to stay in the car until I know where we're going?"

While I was excited to get a puppy, it also terrified me to be out of Oz's house and out in the world. I felt like everyone who saw me could tell that something was broken inside me.

Twisting my fingers together, I nodded. "Can we look at them alone?"

He nodded as he gripped the steering wheel. "I'll see what I can do."

I watched from the passenger seat as he walked up to the house and then stood on the porch. Every few seconds, he looked over at the car to make sure I was okay. If it weren't for Oz, I wasn't sure if I could get out of bed most days. It was still difficult, but he made it easier with each passing day.

Oz came bounding down the stairs and over to the car with a wide grin. Opening my door, he held it open for me. "Are you ready?"

"Yes, but you didn't even tell me what kind of dogs we're looking at." In reality, it didn't matter because I hadn't met a dog I didn't like, but it was driving me crazy to have no idea.

"I know, and there's a reason for that," he said as I followed him around the house.

"What's that?" I tilted my head to the side to look at him while at the same time hearing the sound of puppies yipping happily. I could feel the smile break out on my face.

"Because I wanted it to be a surprise and to keep the excited look on your face all morning."

I had been excited, but it was starting to wane the longer we were away from the house.

"Let's do this." His pace picked up.

I swore he was the most excited out of everyone to get a puppy. Ford was neutral, West was grinning bigger than I'd ever seen him when we left, and Fin was Fin. A puppy did not excite him in the least, but he gave in for me.

I stopped dead in my tracks when I spotted six puppies rolling and jumping around in a pen set up in the backyard. "Oz, oh my… I can't even."

Placing his hand on my lower back, he pushed me closer. "Get in there and pick yourself a puppy."

How was I going to choose?

I stepped over the side of the pen, and all the puppies ran over to me. Sitting down in the grass with all of them vying for my attention, everything else in the world faded away.

"What kind of puppies are these?" I held one that had blue eyes to my chest and snuggled with it.

"Labradoodles. From what I've read, they're one of the smartest dogs on the planet."

Standing with five dogs jumping all over you and one in your hands wasn't easy, but I managed. "How am I going to pick just one when I want them all?"

Oz chuckled as he scratched the puppy in my arms behind the ears. "There's no way in hell Fin's going to let six dogs come home with us. But… I've watched you play with every single dog here, and I think you've already picked."

He looked down at the puppy, who was now resting its face on the side of my neck like he was hugging me.

"Did you see its eyes?" I turned around so he could see the eyes I fell in love with.

"It's sleeping," Oz whispered.

"Can you tell if it's a boy or a girl? I hate calling it, it."

"Um…" he dipped his head and then shook his head. "I have no clue, but I'll ask the people when I tell them this is the one we want."

I was squealing from the inside out at how happy I was. I was already in love and never wanted to put the puppy down.

We started walking toward the house when Oz turned to look down at me. "Do you want to come up with me to talk to them?"

Did I want to? No, but I was going to step out of my comfort zone. "I think so."

I stood back, letting Oz do all the talking to the sweet couple who looked at the puppy with love. I almost felt bad for taking him home with us. When Oz asked if it was a boy or a girl and they proudly stated it was a boy, my mind instantly started racing with names for him.

Max.

Sammy.

Odin.

Riley.

The list went on and on, but none of them fit him.

Once back in the car, Oz started it and asked, "And now shopping?"

"Don't you have to pay?" Throughout the whole time talking to the breeders, we never once paid them.

"I paid them before we went back there," he smirked.

"Oh, that was confident. What if I didn't like any of them?" I bit on the inside of my cheek, trying to keep from smiling.

Tipping his head back, Oz let out a booming laugh that filled the car. I watched as his Adam's apple bobbed up and down. "That wasn't even a possibility. I knew you'd fall in love with one."

Leaning forward, I grabbed my wallet. "How much do I owe you?"

"Zero. It was my idea, and I wanted to buy you a birthday present."

I scoffed because my birthday wasn't for another two months. "You have no idea when my birthday is, do you?"

He glanced over to me and then back to the road with a sly smirk on his face. "It's Halloween."

Wow, he really did know.

He pulled back onto the road and headed in the opposite direction of Willow Bay. "You know it's too bad you didn't pick a girl dog because then we could have bought all kinds of pink things and put them all over the house. Fin would hate it," he laughed.

"Do you really want to piss off the man whose house you're living in?"

"Hey, I pay rent." His tone went high as he defended himself.

"Let's not push Fin too much, or the next thing we know,

he'll be kicking my ass and this sweet puppy here to the curb."

"That's never going to happen. I'm Fin's best friend and have gone through a lot with him. He knows how much you mean to me and would never kick you out."

I was important to Oz?

I mean, I knew I was, but the way he said it made it sound like I was more than a friend—more than his sister's best friend. That's all I've wanted for the last two years.

Luckily, or as unlucky as it was, Oz pulled up in front of a pet store before my mind could start over-analyzing what it meant when he said those words to me.

While we might not have bought a bunch of pink things, I think I bought everything blue in the boutique pet store Oz found. Miraculously, we were the only people in the store, and the saleswoman stayed behind the counter the entire time. This puppy was going to be living the life. He had two dog beds, leashes, collars, and about a million toys and treats.

"Oh my God, he's the cutest thing I've ever seen," Dani cooed from our FaceTime call. "What did you name him?"

"I haven't yet." I scooped the Labradoodle puppy up into my arms and hugged him. He was soft and the sweetest of the puppies we'd met earlier in the day. He kept giving me kisses on the cheek and snuggling his face into my neck. It was like he knew exactly what I needed when I didn't. I only knew that I needed Oz by my side; otherwise, I felt like I couldn't breathe, and I wasn't going back to school at UCLA. I wouldn't be able to function, thinking that creep was out there waiting to attack me again. I was already a walking zombie. I was either numb to the world, or I was feeling everything.

She sat back and asked. "How's Oz treating you?"

"Like I'm made of glass, and if he breathes on me the wrong way, I'll break." I'd like to have thought I wasn't that fragile, but I probably wasn't too far off the mark.

"You look better. I'm sure it mostly has to do with the puppy, but it's nice to see you smile." Dani looked down, and when she finally looked back up, tears filled her eyes. "I was so worried about you. I wasn't sure if I'd ever see you like you are now."

I took in a shaky breath. "I'm not going to lie, it hasn't been easy, but the guys are keeping me entertained, and now I've got this guy." I snuggled the puppy, and he licked my cheek. "So, I've been doing some thinking, and I don't know if I can come back this semester knowing he could be anywhere."

Dani nodded. A tear tracked down her cheek that she

didn't bother to wipe away. "When you're ready, I want you to describe him to me, and I'll do everything in my power to find out who he is and bring him down."

"No," I screamed. "You need to stay away from him."

Oz came running into the room, panting as if he just broke the sound barrier trying to get to me, and he was probably close. "Are you okay?" He knelt in front of me and looked me over.

I shook my head, unable to speak.

Oz nodded like it all made sense to him when nothing in this world made sense to me anymore. Not now, and maybe not ever. Taking my phone, he sat down in front of me. "Hey, Dani. What's going on?"

Dani proceeded to tell Oz what we were talking about as I sat trembling. Once she was done talking, Oz sat still for a moment. His eyes locked on me. "I agree with Lo. You shouldn't go looking for this guy. In fact, you need to stay vigilant about your safety in case he comes after you."

"Do you really think he'd do something like that?" Dani asked with wide eyes.

"I… I can't say. I have no idea how a sick mind like that works, but it's better to be safe than sorry. I would then have to hunt this fucker down and murder him if he touched both…"

What was he planning to say?

I settled my hand on top of his, and his gaze jerked to mine with surprise. "Don't do anything stupid, Dani."

"Hey, where'd you go?" Dani snapped from the phone.

"Sorry," he said, lifting the phone. He stared down at it like he wasn't sure how it got in his hand.

"It's fine, but I hate feeling like I'm missing things. I wish I could come up there, but the team's training is starting on Monday."

I couldn't imagine spending most, if not all, of my free time training like Dani, Oz, and the other guys did. They were all training more now in college than they ever did in high school. College sports were no joke. Fin learned that last season when a shoulder injury took him out for the rest of the season. I hadn't heard if Fin was playing this year, but I assumed so since he was going to practice.

"I wish you were here. Willow Bay needs to step up their soccer team so that you can move here." Oz held my phone up higher and flashed a smile at his sister.

"I'm never moving, even if my two favorite people are there," Dani laughed.

"So, you don't mind if I stay?" I managed to squeak out.

"I want you to do whatever you need to do to make yourself feel safe. If that's living with my brother, so be it."

My cheeks flushed at her words. "It's not like that."

"I know, chica. You're too good for my brother," she giggled.

Oz's eyes closed as if he was in pain. I didn't think Dani realized how much she was hurting her twin brother by always putting him down. I'd heard the stories, but I'd also seen how he hadn't hooked up with a girl in forever. Or if he had, at least it wasn't getting back to me.

"Nah," I shook my head. "He's too good for me."

Oz moved to sit beside me and rested his back against his bed. The puppy walked all over his outstretched legs and then back over to me. Having Oz this close to me was strange. I felt calm and nervous all at the same time. I could feel his body heat rolling off of him, which in turn made me shiver. "Dinner's ready, so we'll talk to you later, Dani."

"Okay," she said hesitantly. "I love both of you."

"Love you, too, sis," Oz responded and hung up the phone before I could say a word. Picking up the puppy from my lap, Oz ran his hands over the soft white and brown fur.

"What's for dinner?" I asked.

"No clue, but for the guys and me, it's whatever's in the fridge. The woman who prepares our meals for us stocked the fridge and freezer today while we were gone getting the puppy. Plus, I thought you wanted to get off the phone, and food is the easiest excuse."

"You don't have to lie to your sister for me. I can handle her."

Oz cocked his head to the side. "Are you sure? It seemed like you got uncomfortable there."

I shrugged. "There's not much that doesn't make me uncomfortable these days. Just when I think life is starting to make sense again, my body gets the chills and flashes from…" I couldn't say the words.

Leaning to the side, Oz nudged his shoulder with mine. "You don't have to say it if you're not ready."

"Thanks." I pulled my knees up and wrapped my arms around them. "I'm not sure if I'll ever be ready to utter those words."

Rolling his head on the edge of the mattress, he looked over at me. "You know what I think?"

"No idea," I said truthfully. I often wondered what was going on in Oz's head. What I wouldn't give to live inside there for a day.

"I think you're too hard on yourself. It's only been a week since you moved here. While I'm not a psychologist, I think everything you're feeling is perfectly understandable. Still, maybe you should see someone to get help."

The thought of talking to a stranger had my insides twisting and turning into knots. I wasn't sure I'd ever be ready for that step.

"Let's feed you and the puppy, and then we really need to figure out his name. What do you say?" He flashed me a smile.

I nodded, feeling hungry for the first time in over a week.

"Hey, Oz," I called as we left the bedroom.

"Yeah?" He looked down at me with a grin on his face.

I gave him the biggest smile I could manage. "You know you're way too good for me, not the other way around, right?"

FIVE
OZ

SEPTEMBER

MY JAW LOCKED as I glared out the windshield, remembering how upset Lo had been when I left earlier.

"Why do you have to go?" Her chin quivered, and her eyes glistened with unshed tears.

"I don't want to, but I have to. I'll be back as soon as possible. I promise." I wanted to hug her and hold her to me, but I had no right, especially now when I was causing her distress.

"Can I go with you? We can take Charlie, and I'll stay out of your hair," she pleaded with me.

Lo and I were inseparable most days, except for when I

was in class and practice. She decided to take online classes and was busy most of the day. Still, I came home for lunch and stayed until I had my next class. Lo would heat up whatever was brought for us to eat and make herself something, and we'd all sit down to dinner together. When she wasn't in class, Lo took care of Charlie and trained him. He was smart as a whip and was learning at least one new trick a day, it seemed.

"You're never a problem, Lo, but this is one instance where I can't take you. I'm sorry. It will only be a couple of hours, and then we can do whatever you want. We can take Charlie to the park or…" I couldn't continue with Lo's tears brimming to the surface and about to spill over at any second.

"Just go, Oz." She turned away from me and wiped under her eyes. While she still had nightmares every night and I ended up in bed with her, Lo was doing better during the day. While I didn't want to leave her, I didn't think it would cause her pain.

I reached out and squeezed her bicep. "I'm sorry, Lo. I'll make it up to you."

"Why can't you tell me where you're going? Are you meeting up with a girl?" She asked, still with her back to me.

"Not a girl." I debated on what I should tell her and then went with the truth, or as much of it as I could tell her. "I'm *meeting up with Dean about an hour from here. It's just a quick meet, and then I'll be right back."*

"That doesn't make sense. I know Dean, and he wouldn't care if I came along."

No, he wouldn't. In fact, I was sure he'd love it so he could find something else to hold against me. I couldn't keep fucking up with Dean, or I'd owe him my life.

"Can you just trust me when I tell you it's best if you don't go? If I didn't have to meet with him, I wouldn't." My hands clenched at my sides with frustration.

Picking up Charlie, she hugged him and buried her face in his fur. "Don't hurry back on my account."

Fucking hell. Doesn't she know I would never do anything to upset her? Seeing her like this was killing me inside, but if she found out what I'd done, I wouldn't be able to look her in the eye ever again, and she'd more than likely want to leave and never come back.

"Maybe I'll see if West can take us to the park or something."

A growl rumbled from my chest. At least Lo picked someone who wasn't interested in her. If she had said Ford, I would have lost my shit and probably killed him before I left. "Lo, don't be like that."

When she didn't turn around to look at me or say another word, I walked up behind her and kissed the top of her head. "I really am sorry."

Now, though, I was going to kill Dean. This bullshit had been going on long enough. If I let it keep happening, he'd never stop, and my parents were starting to wonder where all my money had gone.

Fifty minutes later, I pulled up to a deserted park and shut off my car. Of course, Dean wasn't there yet. He was going to try and drag this out, but little did he know I was going to end it once and for all.

Getting out of my car, I sat on the edge of my hood and waited for the asshole to show up. How would I make things right with Lo when I was only now starting to see progress with her? Would she not trust me anymore after this?

The sun glinted off the hood of a car, signaling Dean's arrival. If he had been here when I pulled up, I wouldn't have been as pissed off as I was, but with each passing second that went by, I kept thinking of Lo and how hurt she was when I left. And it was all Dean's fault.

"Hey, man, you beat me here," he said as he walked around his car with a stupid smirk on his face.

"Don't talk to me like I'm your friend. Friends don't blackmail each other and try to ruin the other person's life," I gritted out. My fist balled up, ready to fly at any moment. One wrong word and I was going to lay into him.

Dean stopped a few feet away from me and crossed his arms over his bulky chest. "Fuck, you're surly today. What crawled up your ass and died?"

"You did, asshole. This is the last time we're meeting up, and the last time I'm giving you money. My parents are starting to question where it's all going."

"That sounds like a 'you problem' and not a 'me problem,'" he said without a care in the world.

"Well, it's going to become a 'you problem' because we're done." I stood, towering over his five-foot ten-inch frame with my six-foot-two body. He was huge for a guy his size and would put up a fight, but I had pure unadulterated rage on my side, and it would fuel me to kick his ass.

"No," he shook his head with a cocky smile on his face that I was about to punch. "That's not how this works. See, you fucked up, and I know your deep, dark, and dirty secret. If you don't want your friends, sister, or the precious girl you like to find out, you'll do exactly as I say for however long I want."

"All the drugs you've been doing have messed with your head because you're not hearing me. I'm done. *We're done.* We will not be meeting again unless it's for me to end your life. Do you understand?"

"So, you don't mind if I tell everyone all the things that you've done? You won't be sweet old Oz anymore when they find out what you'd been up to when you weren't with your friends."

I snapped. That's the only way to describe what happened to me. One second, I was listening to him spout his bullshit, and the next, I reared back and punched him in the cheek as hard as I could.

After that, it was on.

Fists flew, punches landed, and blood spilled, all in a matter of seconds. Rage filled every molecule of my body as I let out all my frustrations with Dean, Tori, Lo, school, and football.

Straddling Dean, I had my arm cocked back and was about to land the ending blow when I looked down at his bloody and already bruised face and stopped. I wasn't the type of guy who hit someone when they were down, and I wouldn't lose more of myself than I already had because of this asshole.

Slamming my hands on his chest, I stood and paced the parking lot, trying to cool down. Once I could finally see straight, I opened my car door before looking back toward Dean. "Don't you ever contact me again, or I will end you, do you understand?" Venom laced each of my words.

There's no way in hell I was letting him ruin my life.

Dean moaned from his spot on the ground but otherwise didn't say anything as I got into my car. I didn't bother to look back at him. If he knew what was good for him, he'd leave me alone.

The drive home gave me time to cool off, but not enough to figure out what to say to Lo or anyone else who asked any questions.

All eyes except for Lo's were on me as I stepped into the house. Everyone looked disappointed in me for a brief second until they got a look at my face. I hadn't bothered to look into the mirror as my adrenaline faded, and the dull ache turned into a full-on throbbing by the time I got home.

Fin jumped up off the couch and followed me into the kitchen. "What the hell happened to you? Do I need to kick his ass?"

A humorless laugh rumbled out of me as I grabbed a bag of frozen peas and placed them on my eye. "I don't need you defending my honor, but thanks. I kicked his ass. No worries."

"Who's? Why did you leave like that, man? Lo has been looking like you were going to ship Charlie off when you got back the entire time you were gone." He leaned in and then looked over his shoulder to make sure no one could hear. "Did you go hook up?"

"No, dumbass. Would I look like this if I did?"

Fin shrugged. "Maybe that's your kink, or maybe if she had a boyfriend."

I tried to push past him, but Fin blocked my exit. "You know who I'm interested in. and I'm not going to do anything *else* to jeopardize that."

"What *have* you done to fuck up your chances?" Placing his hand on my shoulder, Fin looked at me with pain etched all over his face. "Come on, man, you know you can talk to me."

"I know, and I will, but fuck, can't I live in denial for a little bit longer? Once you find out, you won't see me the same way again." I couldn't look at him as I spoke.

Fin let out a low exhale. "Unless you tell me you're secretly in love with me, we won't have any problems."

This fucker. He knew how to make me laugh. Shoving him in the shoulder, I let out a bark of laughter. "I love you like a brother, but nothing more."

"Good, because I would hate to have to kick your ass out of here. I might still because I'm tired of smelling your stinky-ass feet every time I sit down on the couch. You need to either sleep in your bed or on your floor or something because we can't go on like this."

"You're an asshole, man. You know my feet don't stink. It's fucking Ford. Kick his ass out."

"Hey," Ford shouted from the living room. "Not cool."

Fin turned back to me, his face devoid of all humor. "You should probably go check on Lo. West and Ford tried to cheer her up, but nothing they did helped."

I hung my head and nodded. "She was really upset. I'm not sure if she'll ever forgive me for leaving her."

"Hey, it's not like she isn't alone sometimes. You can't be here every minute of every day, but it's different when it's for school. This came out of nowhere, and you wouldn't tell any of us what you were doing. Now you came back with a black eye and busted knuckles." I lifted my aching hand and inspected it. "Coach is going to ream you a new one if you can't catch a ball."

"I know, but this couldn't be helped. I hadn't planned on losing my shit, but…" I shrugged.

"Shit happens. I know." A grin spread across his face. "Now tell me who kicked your ass."

"No one. I kicked his," I answered, pushing past him.

I'd barely hit the hall when Lo and Charlie came running to meet me.

"Oz," Lo cried. "What happened?"

"I got into a fight, but I'm fine."

"Are you sure?" She lifted her hand. It hovered near my face, but then she dropped it.

"Nothing a little ice won't fix. Did you eat? Because I'm starved." I asked as a way to break the tension, but going by the narrowing of her eyes, I had a feeling I'd failed spectacularly. "Why don't we go pick up some lunch and take Charlie to the park?"

"And then will you tell me what happened? Did you and Dean get into a fight?"

"Dean?" I heard Fin, West, and Ford shout all at the same time.

"He was an asshole, and I needed to put him in his place.

It's as simple as that. He got in a couple of good shots, is all, but I'm fine."

"Promise me it won't ever happen again," she demanded. Her blue eyes were somehow both hard and glassed over with emotion.

"I promise."

And I hoped it was a promise I wouldn't have to break, but I had a feeling the actions of my past would come back to haunt me, causing me to lose Lo for good.

SIX
LO

OCTOBER

COMING OUT OF THE BATHROOM, I spotted Oz staring blankly at the television while scratching behind Charlie's ears. He had dark smudges under his eyes from getting very little sleep since I'd moved in. No matter what I said, I couldn't convince him to let me sleep on the couch, nor would he sleep in his own bed even after I offered to build a pillow fort between us.

It doesn't make sense when he ends up in my bed night after night, trying to fend off my nightmares. If I'm comfortable, what's holding him back? I knew something was bothering him, though. He'd been unusually quiet since the night he came home after fighting with Dean. As far as I knew, he hadn't opened up to anyone about what had happened.

He's dead on his feet, and if he kept going like this, he was bound to get hurt while out on the football field. I had to do something.

I moved in front of the TV to get his attention. "Hey, do you want to go with me to take Charlie for a quick walk so he can do his business?"

Before I could finish talking, Oz pushed up on his feet and grabbing Charlie's leash. I kept silent until we'd walked about a block from the house and had turned back.

"You can't keep going like this," I started.

He switched the leash between his hands and looked down at me with scrunched brows. "Like what?"

"You need sleep, and you're not getting enough."

"I'm fine, Lo." He brushed me off.

"No, you're not. So, you're either going to start sleeping in your bed or…" I bit the inside of my cheek, hoping I didn't have to make good on my threat.

He stopped walking, causing Charlie to pull on his leash and jump around. "Or what?"

"Or I'll have to move out. Find a different place to stay." I had nowhere else to stay, and it would kill me if I had to leave. In the two months I'd lived with Oz and the guys, I've grown to love each and every one of them. They took care of me every day when they didn't have to.

"Come on, Lo. You don't want to do that," he said, frustrated, gripping the back of his neck with his free hand.

"No, I don't, which is why you need to agree to sleep in your bed. If you're not comfortable with me being in your bed, I'll sleep on the couch."

"Lo—" he started to argue.

"No," I stopped him, holding my hand up. I knew he was going to turn me down. Again. And I wasn't having it. "You pick. It's one or the other. What am I going to do if you get hurt during practice or a game? What if you can't play football ever again?"

"I'm not West. None of us are. He's the only one who has a shot at playing in the NFL, so if you're so worried, make sure West is getting his sleep."

"What the hell is wrong with you?" I shouted. This wasn't the Oz I knew. He was never an asshole to me.

"You're right. I am tired. I'm sorry, but I don't think sleeping in the same bed is a good idea." He shook his head slowly. He looked like he was close to falling asleep on his feet.

"Why not? At some point each night, you come in there, and once you do, I don't have any more nightmares. Maybe if you fall asleep in there, I won't have any at all," I tried to reason.

"Is that what you're worried about?" he cocked his head to the side. "You want me to sleep with you so that you won't have any nightmares?"

"No, I want you to sleep in there with me because you're tired as fuck, and you deserve to sleep in your own bed. But I also think it might help me not have nightmares as well."

"Have you talked to your therapist about this?"

"No, I haven't. I don't have to run everything by her." My annoyance was clear in my tone.

While I did think my therapist was helping me, the person who helped the most was Oz. I knew it probably wasn't smart to rely on him the way I did, but I couldn't help it. Now here I was, threatening to move out, which would probably set me back more than anything else just to get him to sleep in his own damn bed.

Oz started walking, leaving me where I stood. I wasn't sure if I convinced him or not, but I sure as hell hoped I did because it would kill me if I had to move. My mind raced with trying to figure out something else but came up blank. Once I snapped out of it, I realized I was alone in the street in the dark.

I ran to catch up with him, panting as I sprinted. "Oz, wait." I must have sounded as freaked out as I felt because Oz stopped and waited for me. Only I didn't stop. I kept running until I smacked straight into Oz's chest and wrapped my arms around his waist. It was the first real contact we'd had when I was awake and not suffering from a nightmare.

One of his hands splayed out between my shoulder blades and held me to him. "What happened? Is there someone out there?"

"I don't think so, but I got freaked out when I realized I was standing out here by myself. It brought back…" I started to shake, thinking about it. Just when I thought I was getting better, BAM. It was like I'd been hit upside the head with the reality I was never going to be the same.

"Hey," he soothed his hand up and down my back. "It's going to be okay. I shouldn't have left you alone. I'm sorry."

I held him tighter, wanting to feel safe. Oz Francisco was the light to my dark and fucked up life. "Can we just go home now?"

"Yeah, sure. I am sorry, Lo. I didn't mean to scare you."

Charlie barked, breaking the moment. He was as ready as I was to get home.

I needed to stop thinking of their all-boy house as my home, though. Eventually, I'd have to move on with my life and out of the house. The simple thought scared me more than realizing I was outside in the dark where anyone could get to me.

Putting his arm around my shoulders, Oz tensed but kept walking. "Is this okay?"

"Yeah, it's okay." I hated he needed to ask, but I liked that he asked all the same. "Can I ask you something?"

"You can always ask me anything," he shot back.

"Are you afraid you'll do something to me in your sleep or something?"

"No," he drew out the word. "Well, kind of. I can't control what happens down south when I'm sleeping, and if you woke up in the middle of the night or the morning and were met with my morning wood, I'm afraid you'll freak out."

I couldn't promise him I wouldn't because I might, but it was worth the risk.

"You've been in my bed every morning, and nothing has happened," I tried to persuade him.

"That you know of. Trust me, it's happened, but I've kept away and dealt with it."

Dealt with it? Was he talking about jacking off?

Curious, I asked. "Does it happen because it's morning or for another reason?"

Stopping on the front porch, Oz grinning down at me. "Mostly, it's you, but some of it is because I'm a guy, and it happens. It can't be controlled hence why I've kept my distance."

Reaching out, I touched his arm. It felt so strange to be this close to him when we'd been around each other for years and rarely touched. "I don't want you to keep your distance.

72

If something changes and I feel uncomfortable, I'll let you know." But I didn't see that happening.

"If you're sure," he nodded, looking exhausted.

"I'm more than sure." I took Charlie's leash from Oz and gave him the best smile I could muster.

Oz stood by the front door as I hooked the leash on the hook by the door and started down the hall, then realized he wasn't behind me. "Go get ready for bed, and I'll be there in a few minutes. I need to talk to Fin about something."

"Okay." I swallowed nervously. While I wanted Oz to get some sleep, I was worried I'd bitten off more than I could chew. I went about my bedtime routine I'd started since being here. I put oils in my diffuser to help me sleep. Then I indicated to Charlie to go to his bed where he stayed and watched me as I changed into the most unsexy pajamas anyone owned.

After twenty minutes, I'd laid down and gotten up three times and paced the room waiting on Oz. What was taking him so long? I was close to leaving the bedroom and seeking him out when he slipped into the room.

"Hey," he quietly said, walking over to his dresser and pulling out a pair of what looked to be unworn pajama pants. Without looking at me, he headed back to the door. "I'm going to go brush my teeth and change. Do you need anything?"

For this not to be awkward. "No, I'm good."

Sitting down on the bed, I waited impatiently for Oz to come back inside. The second the door opened, so did my mouth. "If this is going to make you talk to me less than you have been lately, you can go back to sleeping on the couch."

With his lips turned down, he stopped at the end of the bed. "I… I haven't." He paused at the look on my face telling him he was a liar, and nodded before he sat down on the end of the bed. "It's nothing you've done. I'm just stressed."

"You can talk to me about it if you want. I'd much rather hear someone else's problems than think about mine."

Oz turned to look at me over his shoulder with a sad smile. A smile that told me he wasn't going to talk to me about whatever was bothering him.

Patting the other side of the bed, I asked. "Does this have anything to do with Dean?"

Oz moved from the end of the bed to get under the covers, keeping at least two feet between us. Turning on his side with a scowl, he asked. "What makes you say that?"

"I don't know. You've been different since your fight with him. I'm sure whatever happened between the two of you can be worked out." Actually, I wasn't sure about that at all. Whatever went down between them ended with Oz having busted knuckles and a black eye.

"Dean is no friend to me, and he never will be. Hopefully, he'll stay far, far away from the both of us."

"Us? What do I have to do with this? I've never been

friends with Dean. I don't know what you ever saw in him. Then again, up until recently, I never saw why you were friends with Fin either."

I learned Fin just didn't like people in general, but once you were in his circle, you were in, and he'd defend you to the death if it came to it. Once you got to know him, he wasn't all bad.

A dark chuckle rumbled from his lips. "Yeah, no, Dean has no redeemable qualities. As far as I'm concerned, he's out of my life for good."

I felt a 'but' in there somewhere, but he didn't say more. I only hoped one day, Oz would tell someone, either me or Fin, what went down that day when he left me and came back different.

"We should probably try and get some sleep." He rolled over onto his other side, flipped the fan on, and brought the covers up to his chest. "Good night, Lo. If you need anything, I'm here."

I wanted to tell Oz I needed him right then. I needed him to look at me and tell me everything would be okay. Instead, I went with the only thing that I could think of. "Can I hold your hand?"

Oz turned over and looked at me with concern laced all over his face. My hand was already stretched out between us because I needed some type of connection to him tonight. For some reason, I felt as if I was losing Oz, even though he was only inches away.

"Sure," he took my hand in his. "Are you sure you're okay? I promise to never leave you alone out in the dark again."

How was he such a good guy, and yet still so damn mysterious at the same time?

"I'm as okay as I can be, but it's not about what happened out there on the street. I need to start pushing myself; otherwise, I'm going to turn into a recluse. The nights are the hardest." My breath caught in my throat, thinking about how the nights felt like they were trying to suck all the air out of my lungs. The only time I could breathe was when Oz was around. He made the darkness recede. There was a dim light at the end of the tunnel.

"Don't do anything if I'm not here," he demanded. "At least not at first. I don't want to be stuck in class worrying about you."

Bringing my other hand up, I ran the tip of my finger along the vein that ran over the top of his hand and then up his arm. "You shouldn't have to be worried about me. I'm not your responsibility."

Leaning up on his elbow, Oz looked down at me with fire in his eyes. "What the hell are you talking about? The second you came home with me, you became my responsibility, whether you like it or not. You're my friend and Dani's best friend. You're so much more than you realize, and I don't take the trust you put in me lightly."

I was more.

'You're so much more than you realize' kept going on a repeat in my mind. The man before me confused me more each and every day. For years, I'd heard whispers that Oz liked me. Every time I looked in his direction, he was always looking at me, but he stayed away, making me think all the whispers were only rumors.

I'd had a crush on him since the day I saw him but knew he was off-limits as my best friend's brother. I wasn't sure if the stories she told me of him going through the entire female population were true or a sure-fire way to keep me far away from her brother. I didn't question Dani about his reputation, but the way he looked at me now had me wondering what was true.

Could Oz Francisco want to be more than friends with me?

SEVEN
OZ

OCTOBER

"YOU LOOK LIKE SHIT, DUDE," Fin grunted as he came into the kitchen. "I thought finally sleeping in your own bed would help you."

So did I, but for the last week, I'd woken up with Lo draped over my body and the most painful erection each and every morning. I slipped out of bed to relieve the ache, only to give up when I thought of how Lo looked when we showed up at her dorm room. My balls were blue, and my grades were slipping. If I wasn't careful, I'd be benched for my grades.

"Thanks, fucker," I grunted. "I… You know what? Forget it. You don't want to hear it."

Fin shrugged. "I wouldn't have said anything if I didn't want to know. Is Lo still having nightmares?"

"Not nightmares. It's me. I wake up with my dick throbbing, and then I can't do anything about it."

Fin's brows raised. "Why not? Do you need to go to the doctor?"

I couldn't help but laugh at that. A doctor couldn't fix what was wrong with me. "It's nothing like that. It feels wrong to think about Lo and get off after what happened to her. It's like I'm violating her with my thoughts, and now I'm so fucking backed up, man."

"So, think about someone else." He said it like it was the obvious answer to my problem.

"She's who I've gotten off to for the last five years. Do you really think I can change that now?"

Fin doubled over laughing. "Oh my God, you're screwed, dude. You might as well say goodbye to your dick."

"What's wrong with your dick?" Ford asked as he walked into the room.

"Nothing's wrong with it." I narrowed my eyes at Fin, knowing I'd never hear the end of it from Ford.

"Speaking of something being wrong, I need to talk to you." Fin looked to Ford.

"Should I leave?" I wanted to stay because I was a nosy bastard like that.

"Stay for all I care, although Ford might want you to leave."

Oh, now I really wanted to know.

Ford swallowed so loudly I could hear him. "What's going on?" He looked from Fin to me and back to Fin again.

"You've lived here for three months, and rent is due at the beginning of the month. I let it slide up until now, but we're rounding the end of October, and you've yet to pay. Will I be getting any money come November?"

"Um… about that. Things are tight. My mom lost her job, and while she found another one, she's barely able to pay for my tuition." He chewed on his thumbnail as he looked at Fin, waiting for his reaction.

"I'm sorry to hear that." Fin opened his mouth and then closed it as West walked into the kitchen.

West went to the fridge and poured himself some water. "Are we having a house meeting or something?"

"Something like that. Ford can't afford rent, and I was thinking of what he could do to make up for it."

My jaw dropped to the floor. I had a feeling if West hadn't come into the room, Fin would have kicked Ford out but changed his mind because of his boyfriend.

"I'll do whatever you want. I can cook. I'm a good cook, and I can clean. Hell, I'll do everyone's laundry if I have to."

"He can cook," I agreed. "We could stop the service and have Ford cook for us." I shot Fin a smile, wondering if he would agree or shoot Ford down.

"It would be nice to eat something different from the boring-ass shit we have delivered." Fin looked to West, who gave him a nod. "I'll give you money tomorrow to go grocery shopping," he sighed as if it pained him to say it. "If you weren't my friend, you'd be out on your ass. You know that, right?"

If he wasn't a friend, he wouldn't be here, period. I was shocked when Fin asked us to move into the house he bought. It wasn't like what we grew up living in, but for him, it was his escape from his asshole father, who all but tried to fuck him over once he found out Fin was gay. When Fin found out he had money in a trust from his grandparents, he used most of it to buy the house and the rest for tuition. It wasn't millions or anything like that, but Fin was out from under his father's meddling ways. In fact, after his dad tried to tell all of Santa Lucia that Fin wasn't his son and tried to ruin any chance Fin got at getting a job to support himself, he became a pariah. He wasn't going to last long in our hometown. If I lived there, I'd make his life a living hell after all the shit he put Fin through over the years.

"Thanks, man, for giving me this chance. I know I should have come to you," Ford hung his head. "I've been looking for a job but haven't found one yet."

"Just cook for us, and all will be good," Fin mumbled.

"And clean," I chimed in.

"And clean," Fin added. "Alright, meeting's over," Fin clapped. "I'm ready for bed. School, football, and work are kicking my ass, and now this."

Ford and I watched as Fin and West left the kitchen. It wasn't until we heard their bedroom door shut did Ford speak.

"Thanks for letting me stay."

"It wasn't me. It was all Fin."

"Nah," Ford shook his head. "If you would have said no, he would have kicked my ass out to the curb."

Possibly, but I liked Ford, and so did Fin. He was a good guy, and I knew he worried about his mom and being so far away from her during the school year. Last year, he'd been worried about her health, but nothing came of it.

We heard Charlie bark, and then Lo laughed. "How's she doing? She doesn't talk to me much."

"She's doing better every day. I wouldn't take it personally that she doesn't talk to you. She doesn't talk much now to anyone. I wish you could have met her before with Dani."

"Oh yeah, when's your sister coming to visit?" He grinned.

"Don't get any ideas, asshole. That's my sister you're thinking about. She probably won't come up until after her soccer season is over. I'm thinking of maybe going to one of her games if it doesn't interfere with our schedule, but we'll have to see about dates and…"

"Lo," he interrupted. He was a perceptional son of a bitch. "Yeah, I get you, man. I'm going to go crash, but tomorrow night I'm going to make everyone the best damn dinner you've ever had."

"Please let it have some flavor. I'm tired of plain-ass chicken. Eating isn't even enjoyable anymore," I complained. Since moving to Willow Bay, we'd eaten a variation of the same three meals, and I was over them.

"Will do. Good night," Ford saluted me.

"Night." I tipped my chin and headed to my room, where Lo was waiting for me.

"Oz," Lo whispered. "Are you awake?"

I groaned and rolled onto my back. "I am now." I blinked into the darkness. "Did you have a bad dream?"

"No." Her voice shook. "I think I hear someone outside."

I sat up and perked my ears to see if I could hear anything. Just as I was about to tell her I didn't hear anything, there was a thump right outside our window.

"Did you hear that?" She said with a slight edge of hysteria in her voice. Her hand came to my arm.

"You're safe here. You know that. The alarm is set and—"

"People can still break in when there's an alarm. It's not like there's some barrier that comes down over all the entry points when the alarm is set."

"No, you're right. There's not." Had Lo been thinking about some type of shutters coming down for protection? "Charlie?" I called. Maybe he got out of the bedroom, and it was him making the noises.

Charlie jumped up on the bed, nudged me with his nose, and went to Lo, climbing into her lap and giving her kisses. He seemed to be able to feel her anxiety.

Now that I knew it wasn't Charlie, I grabbed my phone off the nightstand and got out of bed. "I'm going to go check it out. Stay here."

"Don't leave me alone." She gripped my arm with a death grip.

"What do you want me to do?" How was I going to protect her if I couldn't get out of bed?

She hung her head. "I don't know. Can't you get Fin to go look?"

Her asking for Fin to protect her struck deep inside of me. Did Lo really think I couldn't keep her safe?

I wanted to lash out at her comment, but I bit my tongue.

"Charlie will keep you safe even if I can't," I gritted out. It came out a little too harshly, but I couldn't take back my words.

I moved to get up off the bed, stumbling over my backpack, when Lo was suddenly standing in front of me. "Please be careful. If something were to happen to you... I would never forgive myself."

"You don't need to worry about me, and anyway, it wouldn't be your fault."

"I'm the one who woke you up." Her voice trembled, and I knew she was close to tears.

"Because you're scared. Now, let me go check it out. Lock the door behind me, and don't let anyone in unless you know it's either me, Fin, or West. Got it?"

I could see her nod in the dark and moved to the door. Turning back, Lo's hands were clasped in front of her chest as she looked my way.

If there was someone outside, I was going to kick their ass for freaking her out. Lo didn't need this shit. She was progressing, and I didn't want anything to halt her recovery.

"Lock it," I ordered as I closed the door behind me.

The second I stepped into the hall, I could hear someone in the back jiggling the door handle. Unsure of what to do, I banged on Ford's door as I walked by his room, hoping he would wake up knowing he had earplugs in.

If Fin and West's room wasn't on the other side of the house, I would have stopped by to wake them up, but I didn't want to waste another second. I wanted to know who the fuck was out there.

Who would dare break into our house?

And why didn't one of us play baseball or at least own a bat? I had nothing but my fists, and if I showed up to practice with busted-up knuckles again, then Coach Kyle would kill me.

I stepped quietly out into the backyard, not wanting to alert whoever was back here to my presence. Keeping close to the house, I spotted a figure near Fin and West's window. Was this someone coming to attack them for being gay? The frat guys at Alpha Mu hadn't taken the disbanding of their fraternity lightly. From the way I'd seen them huddled en masse, whispering as we walked by on our way to class, I was sure they were plotting the demise of my best friend and his boyfriend.

It was too dark outside to see who was at the window. I kept sneaking closer as someone lifted something to the window. I pounced, using one hand to slam the guy up against the wall. With the other, I pressed my forearm to the base of his neck and held him right next to the window.

"What the fuck?" He let out a muffled yell.

Leaning forward, I gritted out beside his ear. "Dean?"

"Yeah, man, it's me. Now let me go." He tried pushing back against me but failed.

I slammed him against the wall one more time before I stepped back, crossing my arms over my chest. "What the hell are you doing here?"

"You won't answer my phone calls." He acted affronted. I'd never understood him. We weren't friends. The only reason he'd been around our senior year in high school was because he knew things about me he shouldn't and was holding it against me. I wished I'd never gotten involved with the asshole. If I hadn't, my life would be so much easier.

"The last time I saw you, I told you with my fists that I was done with you, and yet here you are. Are you stupid? Have all those drugs finally gone to your head, or did you just want another beat down?"

"What the fuck is going on out here?" Fin ground out. He only had on boxer briefs and had his arms crossed over his chest. Dean jumped back, hitting the bushes. "Why are you at my house outside my window in the middle of the night? Are you looking for another ass beating?"

"I did—didn't know it was your window." Dean stuttered out.

"But you did know it was my house, didn't you? And the fact that I've never invited you here makes me wonder why you'd show up looking through windows in the middle of the night. I think you have a death wish."

"No, I just needed to talk to Oz." His entire body shook as he spoke.

Fin took a step forward with his head tilted. "Have you ever heard of this crazy thing called a phone?"

"Yeah, of course." Dean took a step to the side, as if he was retreating. "Yeah, but Oz won't answer."

"And instead of grasping the concept that he doesn't want to talk to you, you showed up here. I knew you were stupid, but I didn't know you were *that* stupid," Fin laughed bitterly.

"Is everything okay?" West asked from the window.

"Except that we have an unwanted visitor, it's fine." He gritted out, but his tone softened as he continued. "Go back to bed, and I'll be there in a minute."

West looked from Fin to me and then to Dean before going back to Fin again. "If you're sure." His eyes came back to me. "Do you want me to go check on—"

I cut him off, not wanting Dean to know Lo was here. Although he probably already knew. I wasn't sure how he found out our address here. It wasn't secret, but no one had been here except for a select few.

"That would be great. I'll *also* be inside in a few minutes." My gaze went to Dean. "After I escort Dean here to his car."

"Do you need help?" Fin asked, taking a menacing step forward.

"I think I got him, but thanks." Grabbing Dean by the neck, I guided him toward the front of the house.

"I can't believe Fin Huntington is gay. How can you live in a house where that kind of shit is going on?"

"Because I don't see it as wrong or dirty. I see it as two

people who love each other, and their love isn't hurting anyone. What I really wonder is how I can live in a world where you keep interfering with my life. If you ever show your face around here again, I'm going to have to end you."

Dean rolled his eyes. "You're all talk."

"Am I? Did you forget everything I said the last time I saw you, now that your face has healed?" I pushed him into the side of his car parked in the street. "I can kick your ass again if it will help remind you that I don't want you anywhere near me or mine again."

"Just give me my money," he demanded.

"Money? I've paid you numerous times, and I told you it was over. I can't keep asking for more. What the hell have you done with what I gave you already?" But even as I said the words, I knew Dean had used it all for drugs.

"It doesn't matter. All you need to know is I need money, and I need it yesterday. If you don't give it to me, I'm—"

"Is someone going to kick your ass?" I interrupted, not caring to hear what else he had to say. "Because I'm fine with that. Happy even. Maybe then you'll stop fucking with me."

"How will you feel when all your friends and family know what you've been hiding from them? Will they see you as the golden boy anymore?"

"I don't give a fuck what any of them think about me." Even as I said the words, I could hear how false my words were. I got in his face and opened his car door for him, letting him know it was time to leave.

"Keep telling yourself that, buddy. I guess we'll soon find out when they hear the news."

"Are you threatening me?" I growled in his face.

"Not at all." He started up his car and put it into drive. "I'm only stating what will happen if I don't have my money in twenty-four hours. You can say goodbye to your little roommate and any chance you have with her."

Before I could respond, he drove off. If he'd stayed another second, I would have dragged him out of the car and pounded his face in.

Looking up at the sky, I let out a silent scream. How was I going to find the ten grand Dean wanted? And what was I going to do when I didn't.

EIGHT
LO

NOVEMBER

I BIT my lip as I watched Oz dress. Not because I wanted
him, but because I needed to break the news that his sister
was bringing someone to our Friendsgiving. We decided to
have a Thanksgiving of our own here in Willow Bay before
everyone went home for the holiday. Well, Fin was going
home with West since he didn't speak to his parents anymore
and I was dreading going home to see my parents. I knew
they'd take one look at me and know something was different
with me. I didn't want to talk about it, and I didn't want to
spend a night away from Oz. We'd been sleeping in the same
bed together for months. He kept my nightmares at bay, and

I was afraid they'd come back while at my parent's house. The only problem was, I couldn't ask him to sneak into my bedroom every night.

Tucking his button-down shirt into his jeans, Oz looked me up and down. "What are you nervous about?"

I let go of my lip. "Is it that obvious?"

"Yeah, you're about to draw blood if you keep on nibbling on your lip. What's up? Do you want me to cancel?"

It was sweet because I knew Oz would cancel the whole Friendsgiving thing, even though Ford had been cooking all morning.

"I don't want you to cancel, but I need to tell you something you probably won't like." I twisted my fingers in my lap.

Leaning back against his desk, he crossed his arms over his chest. "Are you moving out?"

"What?" My brows scrunched together. "Nothing like that. It has to do with Dani."

Oz frowned. "What about her? Is she not coming?"

"Why do you keep assuming the worst?"

"Uh, maybe because you said it was going to be something I wouldn't like."

He had me there.

"She's bringing someone." He quirked an eyebrow. "A guy… that I guess she's seeing."

Oz frowned. "She never mentioned him to me before."

"I know, and that makes me think she likes him. A lot. Maybe don't give him too hard of a time." Dani had only mentioned him to me once, and I could hear it in her voice. Whoever this guy was, he might be the one for her.

Dropping his hands to his desk, he gripped the edge tight enough to make his knuckles go white. "Well, if he's an asshole, I'm not going to let that slide."

"Fair, but I don't think she'd bring him if he's an asshole. She's never had a serious boyfriend—"

"Because they're all assholes. There was no guy in Willow Bay good enough for her." He interrupted. "And probably not in LA either."

I couldn't help but giggle. "You're a good brother, but try to let her have this."

"Fine, he grumbled. "What else is there?" He asked, moving to sit beside me on the bed.

"What do you mean what else?" I ran my fingers through Charlie's hair. I found it was soothing for the both of us.

"There's something else you're worried about, so tell me before my sister shows up with some guy I'm probably going to want to kill." He laid back on the bed and looked up at me.

"It's going to sound stupid," I started, not wanting to tell him.

"Hey, don't be like that." He placed his hand over mine

that was running along Charlie's back. "Nothing you say will sound stupid."

"Fine," I huffed, turning to look out the window. "I'm scared my nightmares will come back when I'm at home with my parents. The only time I don't have them is when you're around."

Crossing his arms behind his head, Oz looked up at the ceiling. "While my parents like you, I'm not sure they'd be on board with you sleeping in bed with me. Hell, Dani might cut off my balls when she finds out where I've been sleeping, and I'm quite attached to them."

"She won't when I tell her you're the only thing that's kept me sane."

He turned his head to look at me. "Are you going to tell her?"

I shrugged, unsure. I didn't want to cause any problems between them, but I would tell Dani if she asked. Or if Oz let me sleep with him back in Santa Lucia.

"You'll have to tell her if you want to stay with us. She's going to wonder where you're sneaking off to every night." He relented, giving me a crooked tip of his lips.

"You don't mind?" I squealed.

"You've got to know by now I'd do anything for you. Including letting my sister cut off my balls to keep you from having those nightmares."

I couldn't contain my happiness. I'd been worried for

weeks about going home, trying to figure out what I was going to do. Releasing Charlie from my lap, I dived to the side and hugged Oz. For a second, he was tense, but as his arms wrapped around me, he relaxed. It felt nice being in his arms. I wanted to dig my nose into his chest and smell his cologne mixed with the soap he used but held myself back.

A loud knock sounded on the door, making me jump. "Dude, you better get out here. Dani's here with some guy," Fin yelled. His loud footsteps could be heard as he stalked to the front door.

Oz sat up and kissed the top of my head. "Let's get this over with."

I slid off the bed, giggling. "It won't be that bad."

"And you can sleep wherever you need to when we go home in a few days. Maybe just don't broadcast it to my parents."

My insides melted. Oz really would do anything for me. "I promise I won't." Snapping my fingers, I pointed to the spot beside me, and Charlie fell into place.

"Fuck, you've got him trained well. I'm damn proud of you," he grinned down at me.

"Thanks." My cheeks heated at his attention. Oz made me feel so many conflicting emotions. Part lovesick and in awe, and equal parts terrified of what I felt for him and what he could do to me *if* I opened up to him more than I already had.

Oz bounded down the hall and didn't stop until he had Dani wrapped in a bear hug.

"Oh, my god, put me down, you big lug," Dani happily shrieked as Oz spun her around. He set her down on her feet, stiffened as he took in the tall, dark, and very handsome stranger standing by the front door.

Dani spotted me and came running with her arms open. "What are you doing all the way over here?" She hugged me gently, like she thought I might break. I wondered if everyone around me would always treat me like a piece of china. I might not be a hundred percent, but I didn't like others reminding me of it all the time. I did that enough as it was.

"Watching your brother size up your man." I pushed away from her. "Thanks for having me be the one who told him you were bringing a guy for dinner."

"Well, I knew he couldn't be mad at you. I swear he looks at you with hearts in his eyes now more than ever."

"You've got an overactive imagination. The only difference is now Oz sees me as broken, and I'm not sure he'll ever see me as whole again."

Dani looked me up and down. "Are you whole?"

"Not yet, but it doesn't help when I live in a house where everyone looks at me like I'm going to have a breakdown at any moment. It's unnerving. And while I might not ever be the person I was before, I've been working on myself with my therapist."

"I know, honey. I'm proud of you. You look good," she nodded her approval.

Oz cleared his throat, causing us to turn around. All the guys stood in a formidable line, glaring at the guy Dani brought. "Are you going to introduce us to your friend or…" he left his sentence hanging.

"Yeah, sorry. I wanted to say hello to my best friend. What's got your panties in a twist?" Dani tried to twist Oz's nipple as she walked by, but he moved out of the way. She took it in stride as she walked to the stranger in the room who had his tense gaze on me while I inched toward Oz. I still wasn't comfortable being around men I didn't know. "Everyone, this is Declan. He's on the men's soccer team at UCLA and one of the best soccer players I've ever seen play the game."

Declan smiled down at Dani. If anyone had hearts in their eyes, it was him. How long had this been going on? Because if I had to guess, he was in love with my girl.

"Hey, everyone," he waved at us awkwardly. "Thanks so much for having me. Whatever's cooking smells divine."

"Hell, yeah, it does. We've been eating healthy for a year, and today we splurge," Fin hollered.

Maybe Fin had been eating healthy for a year, but I'd

taken a break for the summer. Still, it didn't matter; I was down for gorging today and on Thanksgiving.

"On that note, I need to get back in the kitchen before something burns." Ford turned on his heels. "Dinner will be ready in twenty, so set the table, you brutes."

West clapped Ford on the shoulder as he passed by and nodded. "I'll do it. If you leave it up to these two, it will never happen."

Oz scoffed, rolling his eyes. "I know how to set a damn table, but my sister just got here, and I'm meeting her…"

Fin's left brow quirked up as a smirk crossed over his face. "Her what?"

Oz moved, looking ready to tackle his friend. "Shut the fuck up, asshole. What would you do if one of West's boyfriends came around?"

"That's not remotely the same," Fin narrowed his eyes and then followed his boyfriend out of the room.

"Wow, you really know how to clear a room, big bro," Dani laughed. She moved closer to Declan, looking as if she were going to put her arm around his waist, but then thought better of it. Oz was a loose cannon at the moment.

"Sorry, it's not usually *this* bad," I said, giving Declan a tentative smile. His gaze was so intense it had me on edge. Charlie nudged his nose against me.

"Oh my, he's gotten so big," Dani squealed, getting down on her knees to pet Charlie and get kisses. Charlie, being the good boy, stayed by my side until I gave him the signal he could move.

"Did you teach him that?" She asked, rubbing her face into his soft hair.

"She's taught him everything he knows from watching videos on YouTube. It's amazing, huh?"

"No kidding. Maybe you should think about becoming a dog trainer."

"Nah, I don't know what I'm doing," I said, backing up. "I just take bits and pieces from the tutorials I watch and keep trying different things until it clicks. It also helps that Charlie is a smart dog. He practically teaches himself."

"Don't listen to her. She's being modest," Oz put his arm around my waist and smiled down at me.

Dani tensing up didn't go unnoticed by Oz or me. His arm was back by his side in a couple of seconds flat.

Not wanting to contemplate what Dani might be thinking and Declan's intense stare, I needed to get away for a few seconds and breathe. "I'm going to go see if Ford needs any help in the kitchen."

Taking in a deep breath, I leaned against the counter in the kitchen and closed my eyes until I felt someone looking at me.

"Are you okay?" Ford asked from in front of the oven.

"I guess. I don't know. Maybe I've isolated myself too

much because her boyfriend was freaking me out." I shook my head. "It's probably my imagination."

Ford gave me an understanding smile. "He does seem pretty intense. Maybe it's because he's the new guy, and he's intimidated."

Unsure if he was placating me or not, I shrugged, having no clue. I didn't want to grill Dani today, but maybe once we were home for Thanksgiving, I'd ask her what the deal was.

"Do you need any help?" I finally asked.

"Not really, but…" he turned back to look at me and frowned.

"I kinda wanna hide out, and if you give me something to do, then I won't feel so bad," I explained.

He turned back around to all the saucepans on the stove and then back at me. "Can you stir?"

"I'm not incompetent," I laughed. "I mean, unless it needs something special done to it."

"I'm not sure what's special about stirring," he chuckled. "Get your butt over here before you're discovered looking like a deer caught in headlights."

"Ha, ha," I said, moving over to stand beside him. Ford handed me a wooden spoon, and I took over one of the many things he had going on. "Will you be cooking Thanksgiving when you go home?"

"I'll help, but my mom likes to do the majority of the cooking. My brother and sister are both hopeless in the kitchen, and she hates to make it seem like favoritism." He looked down at me and rolled his eyes. "It's always a competition with those two when I could care less."

"I didn't know you had any siblings," I said, concentrating on my stirring when I heard voices coming our way. "Maybe it's because you're the favorite, and they know it."

Ford stopped what he was doing and leaned his hip against the counter. "Let me guess. You're the favorite?"

"For now," I kept stirring and now unable to look at him.

Ford went back to attending to the stove. "Why just for now?"

"Yeah, why for now? Your parents adore you," Oz said, striding into the kitchen.

My shoulders rose to my ears with tension, and my entire attention went to stirring what I realized was gravy. "Once they find out what happened to me, they won't see me as their baby girl anymore. I'll be tainted goods."

"Excuse us for a minute," Oz said as he grabbed me by my upper arm and started to guide me toward the back door. I didn't have it in me to see what Ford thought. I could feel Oz vibrating beside me, but he remained quiet until we were in the backyard and several feet away from the house. He let go of my arm, and when I didn't make a move to look at him, Oz placed a finger under my chin and slowly lifted my head until our eyes locked. "Do you really feel that way?"

"I wouldn't have said it to him if I didn't mean it," I mumbled, averting my eyes from his face that had turned red.

"Lo, no one thinks you're tainted goods, and if they do, they're a dumbass. You didn't ask for this. This happened to you against your will, and anyone with a brain knows you wouldn't have let it happen to you if you had any choice in the matter. You fought, and you survived, and there's absolutely nothing to be ashamed about."

With each word Oz spoke, a tear slipped down my cheek until a river of grief and torment rained down my cheeks. Everything looked blurry as I became a sobbing mess. My knees gave out from under me, and just as I thought I might hit the ground from all the emotions drowning me, strong arms wrapped around me and pulled me against a hard, welcoming body.

"Fucking hell, Lo. I didn't say those things to upset you. You know that, right?" Oz said, his voice frantic.

Unable to answer, I nodded my head against his chest.

The back door slammed, and then all hell broke loose. "What the hell did you do to her?" Dani yelled.

Pulling away, I found Dani moving toward us, and her face had turned red with fury. Her blue eyes were laser beamed on her brother like she wanted to kill him.

Her own brother.

"What the hell, Dani." I moved to get in front of Oz, but

he pushed me behind him as if my best friend would ever harm me.

"What the hell is right. What's going on?" Her blue eyes had never looked so cold as they did at that moment.

"I'm talking to *your* best friend, trying to get her head on straight. Maybe if you'd spent more time worrying about your best friend and less time with this new guy, you'd know how she's feeling. Did you know she thinks her body is corrupted," Oz sounded furious.

Dani moved around Oz to come face to face with me. Her eyes were glassy as she stared at me like she didn't know me. Her face softened as she asked. "Do you really feel that way?"

"I don't want to get into it today. Today's supposed to be fun and not about my problems." I tried to move past her, but Dani blocked my way.

"Your problems are my problems. I love you. You know you're like a sister to me. Have I been a bad friend by not demanding you talk to me about your rape? I was trying to give you space to get your head on right, but if what Oz is saying is true, then your head needs to do a complete one-eighty."

I moved to step back, not wanting the close proximity, except I backed into Oz. His hands went to my shoulders, holding me in place. "Are you telling me a guy will ever want me once they find out I was raped?" Oz's grip on my shoulders tightened. I could feel his body vibrating behind me, but I didn't have it in me to deal with him when Dani was looking at me like she didn't know me. "That my parents won't look at me differently once they find out?"

"No, of course not. No one is going to see you differently," she tried to persuade me of something I knew was completely false.

"That's a lie, and you know it. All of you treat me differently. Not one single person who knows treats me like the person I was before."

I felt his hot breath wash over the side of my neck seconds before his words hit me. Oz only said them loud enough for me to hear. And I knew they were true based on the guttural tone of his voice and the way his hands moved on my shoulders to bring me back to his front and hug me to him. "We treat you that way because of how difficult it was for you in the beginning and still is. But I can promise you I don't see you as damaged or scarred from it. You're still the same beautiful woman I've known for the last five years."

"Stop," I muttered, unable to listen to more from him. I tore out of his touch, needing space.

Eyes blazing, Oz clenched his hands into fists as he spoke the sweetest and most devastating words. "I'm telling you the truth. I've wanted you since the day I saw you, but I knew I wasn't good enough for you. Not then and probably not now or ever, but fuck me if I haven't been trying to make myself a better man in the hope that one day, you'll see me as worthy."

Taking a step toward him against my own volition, it was as if Oz Francisco had a magnet to my heart, and he could turn it on at any moment, bringing me to him. "You are worthy. I'm the one who's not good enough for you."

"Can someone tell me what's going on here," Dani said, breaking us out of our moment.

"What should have been done a long time ago," he said to Dani. Giving her his full attention now. "I should have spoken up the first time you said I wasn't good enough, but you were right." Oz dug his fingers into his hair and pulled. Looking between us, he begged with his eyes. For what, I didn't know, but whatever it was, I wanted to give it to him.

"Am I that bad of a person? Will I ever be good enough?" His voice cracked with raw emotion.

Unable to hold back any longer, I wrapped my arms around Oz and pulled him into me. Hoping my actions conveyed that I thought he was the best man I knew.

"Oz, I never meant to make you feel that way, but I'm not going to lie. You were a manwhore."

Lifting his head from my shoulder, I felt him take in a deep breath. "The keyword in that sentence is I *was*. I'm not now, and I haven't been for a very long time. What do I have to do to prove myself to the both of you?"

Raising my hand, I cupped his cheek. "You don't have to

prove anything to me. I don't know what I would have done without you since I've been here."

"Are you guys a thing now?" Dani asked in utter horror.

I shook my head as I turned to look at her. "I don't know what we are, and I'm not sure when I'll be ready for more, but if Oz still wants me, then yes, we'll be the best damn thing you've ever seen."

Oz took in a shocked gasp. "I'll wait until the end of time if I have to. Take your time," he rasped out. His eyes flicked to his sister. "I love you, but I'm not going to keep my happiness at bay any longer. Maybe one day you'll see that I've changed."

Dani looked down and wiped away a tear. "I know you've changed, but the thought of you hurting her and then you two not being able to be in the same room together kills me."

Oz moved quicker than lightning and had his sister in a big bear hug. "How do you know she won't hurt me?"

"Woman's intuition," she laughed. "Seriously, don't hurt her." Her voice had changed from happy to utterly serious in a nanosecond.

"I would never," Oz vowed as he picked up his sister.

Spinning around in a circle, they laughed. I wasn't sure what this meant, but it seemed to be a step in the right direction.

When I looked back in the direction of the house, Charlie was at the door, looking like he was missing all the fun, with Fin and Declan standing behind him with serious expressions on their faces. I was happy to find Declan's eyes firmly planted on his girlfriend.

Both the guys parted, moving back further into the hallway only for Ford to appear. He opened the door, and Charlie came flying out of the house and towards us. His tongue was flying as he made the short distance.

"Food," Ford called, making Charlie turn in a tight circle and head back inside.

We all laughed as we headed inside to what smelled like the best Thanksgiving ever.

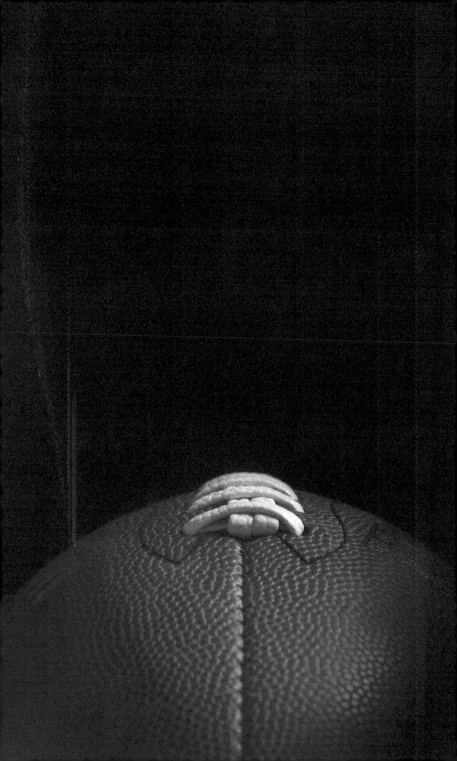

THANKSGIVING

LYING ON MY BED, I groaned from all the food I'd eaten throughout the day. Dani and I couldn't help it, though. Mom made all of our favorites, and we devoured everything in sight until we couldn't eat another bite.

Closing my eyes, I wondered how Lo was doing. She'd been at her parents' house for hours and hadn't returned any of my text messages.

A knock on my door startled me, making me jump, and my food shifted uncomfortably. Turning my head, I found Dani standing at my door with her mouth turned down and her brows furrowed.

I patted the space beside me and asked. "What's on your mind?"

She gave me a lopsided smile. "I've been thinking a lot about what you said at your place on Friendsgiving, and I feel like shit. If you had said something, I would have—"

"I know you would have, and in the beginning, you were right. Maybe you still are. I've fucked up more than any of you know." I turned over and buried my face in my pillow.

I felt my bed dip a second before her hand landed on my back. "Hey, you know you can always talk to me. I won't judge you."

"You will when you know everything," I mumbled into my pillow.

"You're my other half, and I could never hold anything against you. We're young and bound to make mistakes. That's what our youth is for. And I'll never be able to thank you enough for taking Lo in."

Rolling onto my side, I smiled at my sister, who always knew what to say. "I may have done it for purely selfish reasons." Dani frowned. "Only because I've loved her for what seems like forever. I wanted to take care of her and be that person for her."

She twisted her lips up. "So maybe one day Lo really will be my sister."

I looked away as I said. "That's the dream if I don't fuck it up."

"You need to stop talking like that. What you put out into the world comes back to you. If you keep saying you'll lose her, you will." She ran her hand down my arm and clasped my hand.

"I don't even have her yet." I rolled onto my back and stared up at the ceiling. It seemed to be my favorite place to look when I contemplated Lo and me. "I might never."

Dani pushed me, making me nearly fall off my old bed. I sat up, tickling her relentlessly. It was nice to be back in our old house and reverting back to the way things used to be before college life.

"Oh my God, stop before I pee myself," Dani shouted, kicking me in the upper thigh.

"Wow," I let go of her and cupped my balls. "Watch what you're doing. You almost made it so that you'll never be an aunt."

Dani rested her head on my shoulder. "Sometimes you're more dramatic than a girl."

A deep chuckle rumbled out of me. "Oh please, I'm the most chill person you know."

"Lies, lies, and more lies. You used to be the most chill, but now you're always on edge. Why don't you talk to me and tell me what's going on with you?"

For a moment, I thought about opening up and telling her everything that was going on, hoping that my conscience would be a little lighter. Maybe, just maybe, she'd have some advice for me. The second I opened my mouth, I spotted Lo standing at the door and clamped my mouth shut.

Sitting up, I smiled at the gorgeous woman who stood at the entrance to my bedroom and spoke softly to her. "Hey, how was it? You never responded to any of my texts."

Lo looked down for a moment, and when she looked up, tears brimmed her eyes, and her chin was trembling.

"Oh no, honey, what happened?" Dani cried out and ran to her, wrapping her in her arms. They rocked side to side, and for one second, I was jealous of Dani that she got to hold Lo without worrying if it would set her off or back. While we'd hugged a few times, and there was more touching lately, I never knew if Lo wanted it or not.

After a couple of minutes, they broke apart and came to sit on my bed with me. Lo sat between Dani and me, with her knees bouncing.

Turning toward her, I placed my hand on her knee. "Did something happen?"

Sad blue eyes looked up at me. "It was like they could see right through me and everything that was wrong with me. We fought for most of the day, but I couldn't tell them what happened." Her mouth twisted up. "I'm not sure if they'll ever want me to come home again."

Dani scoffed. "You two are sorry sacks of shit who have a cloud of doom over both your heads. You're perfect for each other."

"What are you talking about?" Lo crossed her arms over her chest as she narrowed her eyes at my sister.

"Oz thinks the world is going to crumble around him the second you give him a shot, and you think everyone sees this evil, black oil seeping from your pores which couldn't be further from the truth. You're like... sunshine personified."

"Maybe I used to be, but that's not who I am anymore. You have to understand that I've changed. I don't see sunshine and rainbows all the time. Not that I did before," she muttered. "Now I see all the bad in the world. It's dark and troubled, just like me."

Dani gasped. "Do you know what you're saying?"

"Yes, and as much as we'd all like to forget that I was raped, it changed my life forever. Now it's up to me to decide if I'm going to let it ruin me and my future or if I'm going to rise above what happened and make a difference for other girls who have been through what I've been through."

Fucking hell, I was proud of Lo in that moment. Each day I watched as she came back into herself, blossoming right before my very eyes.

"What does all that mean?" Dani asked softly.

Lo looked at me and swallowed nervously. "I'm going to be a counselor and help others the way my therapist has helped me. If it wasn't for her and the fact that she was raped her senior year of college and what she does with that knowledge, I'm not sure I'd trust her as much as I do. And, of course, Oz. He's been there for me night and day, helping me through the nightmares and never once complained about the sleepless nights."

"Anyone would have done the same," I replied.

Lo cocked her head to the side, her lips quirked up. "You only think that because you're a good guy. None of the other guys were willing to lose endless nights of sleep."

None of the other guys loved her, either.

Dani jumped up off the bed. "How about we stop with all this serious talk, and we go down to the media room and watch a movie?"

"As long as it isn't something scary, I'm down." Lo looked at me. "Are you going to come?"

I shrugged as if I wasn't sure, but I knew if Lo wanted me there, I'd be there.

I smirked at Dani. "As long as it isn't some chick flick that will have my balls shriveling up, I'm in."

"Oh my God, you are such a pig," Dani laughed, and Lo went right along with her. Dani's gaze moved to her friend. "Is it like that at the house?"

"They're not too bad, but I don't watch much with them. Usually, I watch stuff on the TV when they're all at school, and if I want to watch something when they're home, I use my laptop."

"You know, if you ever want to watch something and

everyone is home in the living room, you can. I'll watch whatever with you," I added.

"Maybe," Lo shrugged as she walked down the stairs to the basement.

Even though there were a dozen recliners for us to sit in, we all sat side by side with Charlie in Lo's lap as Dani went through the menu of movies our parents had. It was weird to no longer feel like this was my house or my things.

"Do we want a comedy? Something stupid?" Dani looked up from remote.

"I don't care. Really, it's whatever you girls want to watch," I gave in since I'd more than likely fall asleep watching whatever it was.

"How about an action movie, so we don't all fall asleep from our food comas?" Lo suggested, almost as if she could read my mind.

"That still might not help me. I think I gained twenty pounds between Friendsgiving and today. I'm going to have to run a marathon to work it all off." I patted my stomach.

"If you want, I'll run with you tomorrow morning," Dani said, looking at the movie screen. "I need to keep in shape for spring season."

"Yeah, let's run in the morning. Maybe Fin and West will join us." I looked to Lo. "You can join in if you want."

"Oh, I'd love to run with a bunch of athletes so I can be

left in the dust. I think I'll pass. I'll happily sleep in while you break a sweat out on the streets."

"You know," Dani looked at Lo out of the corner of her eye. "I read that exercise can help—"

"I thought we were done talking about that for the night?" Lo sighed. "Besides, I get plenty of exercise taking Charlie out for all his walks and potty breaks."

Dani held her hands up. "I just thought I'd mention it. I didn't mean for you to take offense."

After a few more minutes of scrolling, Dani made a sound of triumph. "I've got it. We never watched the new Zack Snyder Justice League. Oz will love whatever it is because he loves all those comic book movies, and we get both Henry Cavill and Jason Momoa as eye candy. Win, win!"

I wasn't going to try to school her about what I loved about DC and Marvel movies. I'd been trying to get her to understand my whole life, and if she didn't understand after twenty years, she never would. At least it was a movie I could get behind.

"Oh, wow, it's a long one. We might actually need to get a snack during it," Lo laughed.

"What else are we going to do?" Dani huffed.

She seemed a little on edge this weekend, and I wasn't sure if it was because she didn't like the idea of Lo and me eventually becoming an 'us' or if it was something else.

Maybe she was having problems with her boyfriend, or maybe she was just missing him since they were spending over a week apart. The next time we were alone, I'd ask her about it. Just because I was in love with her best friend didn't mean I wanted a wedge to come between us.

"I'm down." I got up and grabbed a couple of the blankets from the closet and each of us a water bottle. Sitting back down, I threw the other blanket at Dani and then covered both Lo and me with the other blanket. Charlie's head peeked out for a second, and then he went back under the blanket to nap.

Rolling my head to look over at Lo, who still looked a little sad, I tried to think of something that would make her happy. "What did your brother and parents think about Charlie?"

A big smile swept over her face. "They loved him. He showed off for them and did all his tricks. They now think I should be a vet." She rolled her eyes. "I don't think they realize vets aren't the ones who train dogs."

Placing her hand on Lo's arm, Dani asked. "Did you tell them what you want to major in?"

"Not yet. I'm not sure if my parents even realize I'm not at UCLA anymore. They're so clueless. I guess they'll figure it out when I graduate," Lo chuckled, but there wasn't an ounce of humor in it.

"Do you think you'll start going to class or are you planning to do next semester online?" Dani asked.

I could see Lo tense at the question. It kind of sounded like a dig. Maybe Dani wanted Lo back at UCLA with her, but she had to know that wasn't going to happen. The guy who raped Lo hadn't been caught. Dani had mentioned numerous times how she hadn't seen anyone like who Lo described.

"I'm not sure. When I get back, I'm going to talk to my therapist about it, and we'll decide what we think the best route will be for next semester, but I do plan to be in class for our junior year. I'm just not sure if I'm ready yet." Lo spoke the last part so quietly it was difficult to hear her.

Placing my hand on her leg over the blanket, I let her know I supported her in any way I could. "You've come a long way, but if you're not ready, don't push it."

"Thanks," she shifted the blanket until my hand was on her bare leg, and then she covered it up again.

I wasn't sure what she was doing, but whatever it was, I was down for it. I felt like I was some kid in middle school or even elementary who was fulfilled by the smallest of gestures from the girl he liked. When Lo picked up my hand and laced our fingers together, I almost fist pumped; I was so overjoyed.

Money definitely didn't buy you happiness. It was the

simple things in life, like when the girl you loved held your hand.

We sat hand in hand for the rest of the movie, and it was one of the best nights of my life.

DECEMBER

LO WALKED into the bedroom in her barely-there pajamas, and my dick took notice. Oh, he always noticed, but tonight he wasn't hiding how he felt about seeing Lo's long, lean legs and her perky breasts that were barely covered.

"Are you happy everything is over, and you can finally relax?" She asked as she climbed into bed.

"Fuck, yeah. We barely won the championship, and while it doesn't mean much to me, I know West needs it to make it to the draft, so I'll do everything in my power to make that happen."

Her hand brushed along my arm. "That's sweet of you."

"He's a good guy, and Fin loves him. Why wouldn't I?"

She shrugged. "I really like West and Ford."

"Does that have anything to do with all the food he's been cooking just for you? Now that the season is over, I think I'm going to join you once a week for a cheat meal. That is until I start to get fat." I patted my six-pack and pushed it out to make myself look fat.

"You're never going to be fat. Even when you weren't eating as healthy as a horse and working out all the time, you were still in good shape."

"Oh?" I raised an eyebrow. "You noticed?"

"You know I noticed. Anyone with eyes could see," she giggled, and it was music to my ears.

"I don't care about any of them. I only care if you like what you saw." I flexed my pecs, and it had the desired effect. It made her laugh again, and I saw the spark of want in her eyes. It was something I was noticing more and more with each passing day. I wasn't going to push for anything more than what Lo was ready for, so she was going to have to make all the first moves.

Her gaze ran over my bare chest. "I did and still do like what I see. You're one fine male specimen if I do say so myself."

"But what you're saying is you won't like me if I get fat?" I cracked a grin.

"I would still like you," she spoke quietly as she moved

up the bed and rested her head on my shoulder. "Would you like me if I was fat?"

"Without a doubt," I told her. I was sure there was nothing that could make me not like Lo. She'd grown from a skinny teenage girl into a woman in the amount of time I'd known her. She had curves where she didn't use to that drove me wild, and I dreamed of one day running my hands along each one of them and tasting every inch of her skin with my tongue.

"You know, sometimes I see you looking at me like you want to devour me, and while it scares me, it is also exhilarating." Out of nowhere, her hand landed on my knee. "Are you ever going to act on it?"

"Only after you show me that you want it, and I know without a doubt that it's what you really want." The thought of Lo rejecting me or freaking out has me scared to death to touch her in the most platonic of ways half the time. If I started something and she relapsed, I'd never forgive myself.

She swallowed, looking like she was trying to get a jagged piece of glass down, and then tentatively reached out for my hand. I let her take it, seeing what she was going to do.

She placed my hand on her breast and could feel her rapid heartbeat. Closing my eyes, I tried to calm myself down. My blood slowly started to boil, and with each second I touched her, I was close to detonating.

Even though she put my hand on her, I wasn't satisfied

with the knowledge she was ready for what I wanted to do to her. If I started, would I be able to hold myself back unless she told me to stop?

When her chest started to heave, I tried to pull my hand away. "You don't have to do this if you're not ready."

"That's not why I'm breathing so heavy. It's because I've wanted this for so long, and now that it's happening, I can't believe it. I'm not thinking…" Her eyes locked on me. "I'm not having any bad thoughts. They're all *very* good. I want you to touch me more. To make me feel good."

"If I do anything you don't want, I need you to tell me. The thought of you seeing me as someone capable…" I couldn't even utter the words. The thought made me sick to my stomach.

"That will never happen." She picked up my other hand and placed it on her other breast, and it was like someone else took over my body. My thumbs smoothed over her pebbled nipples, and my hands cupped and massaged her full tits.

"I've dreamed of touching you like this so many times." My eyes stayed glued on her big blue orbs that I could easily get lost in.

Lo let out a breathy sigh as she ran her hands over my shoulders and down my chest. "Kiss me, Oz. Please, please, kiss me. Show me this is real and not some dream."

Sliding my hands down to her waist, I pulled Lo onto my

lap, and nothing felt more perfect. Lo was my destiny, and I'd fight heaven and hell to keep her in my arms like she was in that moment.

Cupping the side of her face, I rubbed my thumb over her flushed cheek and her full bottom lip. Leaning in, I brushed my mouth against hers. A shot of electricity ran through my body and bounced around inside me as I tilted my head and licked along the seam of her pretty pink lips.

All I could think about was tasting her. And once our mouths touched, I knew I'd never be the same. Lo Carmichael tasted like my reward and my demise.

Our tongues swirled together as her hands traced over my arms, shoulders, and chest. With each touch, my cock grew and ached, tenting my shorts begging to be let out. I was going to need a seriously long cold shower after this.

Each place she touched me set my body on fire. Her fingers slid up the nape of my neck and buried themselves into my hair. She guided me where she wanted me, angling me as she deepened our kiss and explored every inch of my mouth.

Pulling back, she panted as she looked down at the tent in my shorts that was between us.

Leaning forward, she rested her forehead against mine. Her minty breath washed over me as she spoke. "That was epic."

"I have to agree." I brushed a chaste kiss on her kiss-swollen lips. "It would have been greatly disappointing if we had no chemistry after all this time."

Her blue eyes widened as she giggled. "It would have been bad if you were a bad kisser, and then I had to turn you down."

"But instead, you're perfect for me." I blurted out before I could second-guess myself.

"If anyone here is perfect, it's you." She ran her hand along my abs. When she looked back up at me, her eyes were the color of a raging storm. "Your body is perfection."

Running my hands over her shapely hips, I cupped her ass cheeks and held on. "It is you who's perfect. I can't get enough of your curves."

She smiled shyly down at me. One of her hands smoothed down my back. "Do you want to see all of me?"

"I would love nothing more," I answered back without thought. Lo was barely wearing anything as it was. I could feel the heat from her pussy through my shorts and the thin fabric of hers.

"Will you take my clothes off me?"

It was like I was living in a fantasy. How could this be real?

"It is real. I want this with you, Oz. I want to be able to feel your touch on every inch of my body when I go home tomorrow for Christmas. It will be the only thing keeping me sane when I know you're gone, and I can't get to you." Her hands moved to the hem of her shirt, but I stopped her. Fuck me and my morals.

"Are you sure we're not moving too fast? This is the first time I've touched you and…" Fuck, how did I say this without making her remember the worst night of her life?

Placing her hands on top of mine, Lo dragged her tank top over her head. Her beautiful, full breasts bounced, making me speechless. I was putty in her hands. "What does it matter if it's the first time you've touched me? We both want this. You can't deny it." Lo palmed my erection through my shorts, and I let out a guttural groan.

"If you keep your hand there, I'm going to embarrass myself," I only half-joked.

She stroked me once and then halted, gripping me tightly in her tiny hand. "Tell me what else you were going to say."

"Say when?" I could barely remember my own name, let alone remember something I'd said at some other time.

"When you said tonight is the first time you've touched me. You were going to say more but didn't. I want to know what it was. If you tell me, I'll happily pull you out of your shorts and give you a taste."

What kind of taste?

My nostrils flared, and my eyes widened at the thought. I'd give anything for Lo to taste me.

Her words pretty much gave me the answer I was looking

for, but I needed to know. Lo's answer would determine how the rest of this night would go.

"Before…" This was harder than I thought it would be to ask since I didn't want to fuck this up. "Before August, were you a virgin?"

There. I said it. It wasn't eloquent, but neither was I.

She bit down on her bottom lip, and the sight drove me crazy. Using my thumb, I pulled it out from between her teeth and smoothed my thumb over it. "I feel like whatever answer I give will be the wrong one."

"There's no wrong answer, but it's something I need to know." If her only experience was with the night of her assault, then we needed to take this slow. Very slow.

"I wanted to wait for someone special," her eyes locked with mine, and I read what she couldn't say. She was waiting for me.

"But," I said softly, needing her to say more.

"I got drunk one night last year at a party. He looked so much like you. He had blond hair that wasn't quite as light as yours, and he had brown eyes instead of blue, but," she shrugged. "I think I had beer goggles on, or I just wanted it to be you so bad that I went through with it."

My chest vibrated with the growl I was holding inside. She wanted it to be me and then… no, I couldn't go there. Not now.

"Hey," she placed her hand on my chest, and my heart

immediately slowed down and then sped up from her touch. "It was you I wanted and who I pictured. It wasn't bad, but it wasn't good either."

"Did he know you were a virgin?" I growled out. She looked away, giving me my answer. "As much as I hate that you were with another man, it might have been better if he knew."

"And then I would have had to explain why I was willing to give it up to a stranger," she raised an eyebrow. "I don't think so. Do you think less of me now?"

"No, I don't. How could I? You've heard about my reputation since the moment you became friends with Dani, and I never even showed the slightest bit of interest." A lump in my throat formed as I prepared to tell her something that could very well end the night. "And I haven't exactly been a saint these last five years."

Lo let out a shaky breath. "When's the last time you were with someone?"

My stomach bottomed out. I didn't want to lie to her, but I also didn't want to tell Lo the truth, either. Closing my eyes, I told her before I chickened out. "Eight months ago. It was a one-night stand that meant nothing."

Lo cupped my cheeks with both of her hands. "It's okay. How were you to know this was ever going to happen?"

Leaning forward, I rested my forehead against her chin.

"I wish I could take it back. Take back every single woman I've been with and waited for you."

Pulling back, she kissed my forehead like she's done it a thousand times before now. Touching and holding each other felt so right, unlike anything before. I knew Lo was the person I was meant to spend the rest of my life with.

"Does it help to know you have me now?" she asked quietly.

"Do I, though?" I was one step away from losing her, and I felt it in my bones every day. If Dean showed up and spilled what he knew, or if Lo saw Tori and she blabbed because I wouldn't put it past her.

Lo wrapped her arms around me, holding me tight as if she was trying to comfort me when it was me who should be helping her. "If you want me, you can have me. We've both wanted this for so long."

"I want you more than words can express." The feel of Lo's breasts pressed against my chest and her hot pussy directly on top of my cock was driving me mad. How had we gotten so off track?

Grabbing my face in her hands, she held me there. "I want you to look at me like you used to and not as a victim. Can you do that?"

"All I see is a strong, beautiful woman who I've never wanted more in my life than I do right now," I told her truthfully. "But I want our first time to be special. Let me take you out on a proper date, maybe go out to eat instead of having Ford cook for us."

A smile blossomed on her face. "I'd like that. A lot. We can still keep kissing, can't we?"

"You'll be lucky if I let you up for air before you have to leave tomorrow."

Her smile turned into a deep pout. "Why is your family so awesome and going on a family trip? I hate that I won't see you for a week."

Picking her up and laying her down on the bed because she was too tantalizing on my lap, I moved to lie beside her. Her brows puckered. Placing kisses along her brows and down her nose, she slowly started to smile again.

"I'll miss you too, you know. A week without you in my arms will be hell." I smoothed my hand down one side of her jaw. "I'll plan something special for when we get back. If we're lucky, we might even have the house to ourselves a night or two."

She nodded, running her silky soft hand up my ribs, and demanded. "Now kiss me like you mean it."

For the rest of the night, my lips never left Lo's. It was the single hottest night of my life, and all we did was kiss.

ELEVEN
LO

JANUARY

FLIPPING MY BLINKER ON, I turned onto the street to what now felt like home. Santa Lucia and LA aren't my home any longer. No, Willow Bay, and living in a house with four surly men was my home. From the moment Oz dropped me off at my parents' house on Christmas Eve, my skin had been itching to leave Santa Lucia, but I held out knowing Oz was in Aspen with his family until after New Year's Eve. I wanted to leave yesterday once I knew he was home, but I waited an entire twelve hours before I hopped in my car and drove back to Willow Bay.

Oz's car was in the driveway, along with Fin's SUV and a

strange car I'd never seen. Parking out on the street, I left my bags and Charlie in the car and started up to the house until I heard yelling coming from the backyard.

Slinking through the grass, I edged around the side of the house, hearing Oz yelling, unable to make out exactly what he was saying. A female voice overtook the conversation. She sounded vaguely familiar, but not really.

Who the hell was Oz fighting with?

"You told me you were getting an abortion!" He yelled, sounding frantic.

An abortion?

Moving closer, I caught sight of Oz with his hands gripping his hair, pulling at the long blond strands. His usually tan face was pale as he paced the yard in tight strides.

Standing in the middle of the backyard was a girl with sleek red hair and skin as white as snow. She was thin except for her large protruding belly.

She was pregnant. Very pregnant.

"Well, I changed my mind, and you're going to have to help me pay for the delivery, along with child support," the girl said with a snap.

"What? No, there's no way. We had sex once, and…"

I didn't hear what else Oz had to say. I couldn't. Every fiber of my being started to crumble as what he said clicked into place. Was this what Oz had been worried about for months? No, it couldn't be. He thought she'd terminated the baby she was carrying—a baby that was his.

Running to my car, I hopped inside with a barking Charlie trying to get into the front with me. My hand shook as I tried to turn the key in the ignition, but it was impossible because I was shaking so badly. I didn't know what to do. I needed to get out of there, but I was without any place to go. This was my home, and now it was ruined.

A soft knock sounded on my window, making me jerk back and slam against my seat as I yelped.

Another knock and my name was called again from a growly voice. "Lo, are you okay?" Looking up, I saw Fin looking in through my window with his brows furrowed and a frown on his face. "What's going on?"

Shaking my head, I breathed in a calming breath and turned my car on. Rolling my window down, the cool air hit my tear-streaked face.

Fin looked toward the house and back again. "Did you and Oz have a fight? I thought you were coming home next week."

"I was, but I didn't want to wait, and then I came back to… to…" I pointed toward the backyard.

"What happened? Whose car is that?" He asked angrily.

"I don't know who, but she's pregnant."

Fin's eyes went wide. "It's not mine."

I wanted to laugh when I thought I'd never laugh again. "I wasn't accusing you. I know you've been with West."

"Good, good," he nodded. "I've been with girls, but not in a long time. If West..." he swallowed harshly and then clenched his eyes closed. "Is it Oz's?"

I couldn't answer him. I nodded instead, and more tears streamed down my face. "I need to go."

Leaning into the car, Fin touched my hand that was on the steering wheel. "Where will you go? Back to Santa Lucia? That's a lot of driving for one day, and you're upset. Why don't we go inside and talk? I can make Oz go somewhere else if you want."

I couldn't do that. I didn't know if I'd ever be able to look at Oz again. "I can't right now, but I also can't deal with this. I thought... we were going to be together, and now... I'll go to a hotel," I nodded, deciding on my plan of action.

"Hey, I didn't know, but I think you should hear his side of the story. Oz has loved you since the moment he saw you, and I know he hasn't been with anyone in—"

"He's been with someone. He was with her. I heard him admit it was a one-time thing, but that one time turned into some girl in the backyard getting pregnant. How can I deal with that? How can I..." My throat closed up.

"Do you want me to kick his ass?" My chin started to quiver. "You know I'm going to have to tell him you were here, and then he's going to call you, so you might as well stay here."

I knew it wasn't healthy to run from my problems, but this wasn't fair. Just when I was starting to get trust in myself and men again, this happened.

"Can you hold him off for a day or two? I need time to wrap my head around... I don't even know what. Everything."

Hanging his head, Fin let out a groan. "I'll do what I can, but he's determined, and once he finds out you know whatever the hell is going on, he's going to freak out."

Standing up, Fin hit the roof of my car. "You better go if you want to get out of here before he finds you sitting out here crying."

I did and didn't want to go, but I knew I had to leave for myself; otherwise, I was going to give into Oz when I should listen to what I needed.

"Don't think badly of me." My voice trembled on every word.

Fin's face softened, and he gave me a sad smile. "I would never. I've seen the way you two have looked at each other for years. This might seem insurmountable right now, but I know you'll get past it because you both love each other."

"If he loved me, why is he back there with someone he got pregnant?"

Fin blew out a breath. "Because men are stupid, and sometimes like it or not, we're ruled by our dicks."

That didn't make me feel any better. Who was to say he wouldn't be ruled by said dick again?

Putting my car into drive, I patted Fin's hand. "Thanks for caring, Fin. It means a lot."

AN HOUR LATER, I was in a hotel room in the neighboring town of Loganville with Charlie in bed with me, and the covers pulled up to my chin.

Charlie licked my tear-stained cheek as he tried to comfort me, but there was nothing that was going to make me feel better. Not now. Not for a long time.

My phone started ringing, and I knew without looking it was Oz. I was surprised it had taken him this long to call. When I didn't answer, the phone started ringing all over again. By the third time, I picked up my phone and slid the bar to turn it off. If I had to listen to it one more second, I would lose what little I had left of my sanity.

"What am I going to do, Charlie?" I cried.

I couldn't call Dani and talk to her about it. While she seemed to accept the notion of an *if* between Oz and me, I knew this was exactly what she was afraid of happening. Realizing I couldn't go back home to Santa Lucia because

Dani was spending the next week at her parents' house, and she would know something had happened between Oz and me was another blow. I couldn't risk their relationship, so I needed to figure out what I was going to do. Did I find my own place here or find someplace entirely new where I wouldn't be faced with the man I loved and possibly his baby mama?

The thought of coming face to face with her sent me into another round of hysterics that had the person in the next room knocking on the wall. I banged back, wanting to yell 'fuck you,' but all I did was sob and fall back onto my bed.

The one person I wanted to talk to I hated at that moment. How could you hate someone so much and also love them at the same time?

That thought ran through my head over and over again until I passed out with a sticky face on a wet pillow.

TWELVE
OZ

JANUARY

IT HAD BEEN two days of me calling Lo every ten minutes and her not answering. Running my hands down my face, I groaned.

West flopped down on the couch beside me. "She's still not answering?"

"She turned off her phone, but I keep hoping she'll turn it on, and my call will go through. I'm pathetic, aren't I?"

"No, I wouldn't say that, but you should have been honest with her. If you had told her what was going on with you, she more than likely would have understood."

"You really think that?" I laughed darkly. "If some chick

had shown up saying she's pregnant with Fin's baby, what would you have done?"

"Chopped off his nuts," he growled out.

Fin threw himself into the recliner and kicked up his feet. "Whose nuts are you chopping off?"

West leaned forward and looked at his boyfriend. "Yours if some girl shows up pregnant."

Fin rolled his eyes. "Not that again. You really don't expect Lo to forgive you so quickly, do you? You didn't see how upset she was."

My blood boiled at Fin not convincing Lo to stay here so that I could talk to her. Instead, he sent her on her way, and now I'd be lucky if she ever spoke to me again.

"No, I didn't get to see her because you told her to leave, and now she's turned off her phone. I don't even know where she is," I growled out.

"I told you she said she was going to a hotel that day. Where she is now, I can't say," Fin shrugged. "Have you talked to Dani?"

I couldn't flat out ask where Lo was and make it seem like she was missing. All I knew was they weren't hanging out.

"Do you think I need to call around to the hospitals? What if something happened to her, and she's on the side of the road somewhere hurt?"

West patted my knee. "You can't think like that."

"I'm going out of my mind with worry. Do you think

she'll ever talk to me again?" I buried my hands in my hair and pulled, trying to get some relief.

West shifted to look at me. "I'm not a fortuneteller, but eventually, I think she won't be as hurt, and she'll listen to you."

Slamming the footrest down, Fin's feet hit the floor and his elbows rested on his knees. "Why didn't you tell us?"

"What would be the point?" I shrugged. "I thought she had an abortion, and the situation was over until she showed up wanting money. Money, I don't have because…"

My words were cut off when Lo opened the front door with Charlie by her side. I jumped up and ran to her side. "You're back."

Lo didn't look at me. Instead, she moved to stand in front of Fin and smiled down at him. "If it's okay with you, can I sleep on your couch until I figure out what I'm going to do? I can't stay at that hotel any longer."

Fin's gaze moved to me and then back to Lo. "This is your home, and you can sleep wherever you want." He smirked. "Except mine and West's bed."

Lo smacked him on the shoulder and giggled. "You're not my type." They both looked over at me, but it was Lo who took her eyes off me first. "Thank you for letting me stay. I'll try to stay out of your hair and figure something out soon."

Fin stood and took Lo's bag from her like he was an actual gentleman. If I wasn't in shock from Lo showing up, my jaw would have hit the floor. "The basement isn't finished, but I'm sure we could get you a bed down there if you want. You could have it all to yourself down there."

What the actual fuck? I wanted to murder my best friend. If Lo stayed downstairs, it would be disastrous.

"I'm not sure I can handle being down there in a dark open space, but thank you for thinking of me." She fidgeted where she stood. I hated that I'd made her uncomfortable in a place that had been her sanctuary.

West stood and stretched his arms over his head. "I'm tired and ready for bed." He reached out for Fin's hand. "Are you coming with me?"

Fin smiled devilishly. "I can never say no to you."

"Oh, I didn't mean to kick you out of the living room. You can stay in here. If it's better, I can make a pallet on the floor, so you can have the couch."

"We're not letting you sleep on the floor, and I do want to spend time with him. Alone. Oz has been unbearable to live with the last couple of days, and now that you're both under the same roof, maybe he'll..." he shook his head. "I don't know, but anything is better than what he's been like."

Lo's gaze darted to me before she patted West's arm. "I'm not ready for that, but I won't hold you back from being with your love. Now, if you don't mind, I'm going to take Charlie for a walk and then go to bed. I haven't slept much since... well, since I left here."

The dark smudges under her eyes let me know she wasn't lying about not sleeping since she was last here. I hadn't either. I was too used to having her in bed with me, her soft skin brushing against mine during the night, and her inevitably curling up against my side to sleep with her head on my shoulder.

I should have demanded that my parents invite her to Aspen with us. It wasn't anything new. Lo had been on many vacations with us, but for some reason, they wouldn't budge. And Dani was no help since she couldn't bring her boyfriend, Declan.

"Don't worry about that. We'll figure something out for you soon. In the meantime, we'll leave you to get settled back in." The way West smiled at her let me know Lo was a part of the family now. He hadn't been happy to hear about what happened when he returned home. Neither had I, but this was my fault. If only I'd kept my dick in my pants, none of this would have happened.

"Thanks, guys. I'll try to keep quiet." She looked down at her shoes as if she was an inconvenience when she wasn't even close. I was the problem. Maybe I should find someplace else to sleep or make a pallet in the basement to sleep on instead of making Lo sleep on the couch for the foreseeable future.

I watched as West and Fin traveled down the hallway and into their bedroom. When their door clicked shut, I turned to Lo. "You don't have to sleep on the couch. I'll sleep on it tonight and for however I long I have to until you forgive me."

Instantly, her hands went to her hips, and her eyes narrowed. "Who said I'll ever forgive you?"

Hanging my head, I nodded. I understood she was upset with me, but I didn't cheat on her, even if it felt like I did in my heart. "I know you're not ready for it, but I hope you'll let me tell you my side of the story."

"You got a girl pregnant. What more can you say?" Her voice rose with each word she spoke.

"I'm not with her. It was-"

Lo's hand shot out, and she shook her head. She looked at me with glassy, angry eyes. "I don't want to hear it. Not now and maybe not ever."

"I'm sorry, Lo. You have no idea how sorry I am. If I could turn back time, I'd fix so many things."

She nodded, and Charlie nudged her hand. He always knew when she was upset, and I knew I needed to step down. I wouldn't win any points if I made her listen to me now.

Lo started for the front door, and I remembered she mentioned needing to take Charlie for a walk.

"Do you want me to come with you? I promise I won't talk. I'll just be there for support."

She didn't even bother to look at me as she spoke. "A lot has changed since you last saw me. I don't need you to protect me anymore."

"I know you don't. You never did, but I still want to be there for you in case you need me. I'll hang back, and you'll never know I'm there."

She let out an irritated sigh. "It's a free country."

I wanted to fist pump. It felt like a step in the right direction, even if she didn't want me there with her. Or maybe it was just delusional desperation on my part.

Without speaking, I followed behind Lo and Charlie as she took him on a leisurely stroll. I swore she was dragging it out because I was not dressed appropriately for the chilly night air. Maybe she hoped I'd freeze to death out here.

While she may have said she didn't need me, I saw Lo tense up a couple of times and then look over her shoulder to see if I was still behind her. When she turned around and passed me, I wanted so damn badly to reach out and touch her. Lo's mouth was turned down, and her eyes reflected the pain I'd put her through. I'd never hated myself more than I did at that moment.

How was I ever going to get her to talk to me, let alone forgive me?

As Lo's feet hit the driveway, she turned around but didn't look at me. "Did you mean it when you said I could sleep in your bed?"

I laughed, but it was without humor. "It's as much your bed as it is mine. I only lived here a couple of months more than you, but you've slept in it more than I have."

"I've taken advantage of you, and for that, I'm sorry, but I would appreciate it if you let me sleep in your room for the night. Tomorrow I can figure out my next step." She didn't give me time to respond before she was at her car, pulling out her bags and Charlie's stuff.

"Let me get that for you," I said as I took the bags from her. "And for the record, you're not taking advantage. I want you here for as long as you want." I kept the word forever out, knowing she wouldn't appreciate it.

"I shouldn't be saying this to you, but I want to stay here. This is the only place I feel like myself. Tomorrow I'll go down to the basement and see how habitable it is." Her eyes flicked up to mine, and then she looked down at Charlie and ran her fingers through his curls. "If you don't want me to live here, say so now, and I'll be out in the morning."

I took a step toward Lo, but when she took two steps back, I stopped. "I want you here, even if you hate me. I'd rather you lived someplace where you feel safe and for me to move than anything else."

A tear slipped down her cheek. "How did we get here?"

Emotion clogged my throat, and I wasn't sure if I was going to be able to speak. "I fucked up. I should have told you what was going on with me, but I thought you had enough on your plate. And…"

She tilted her head, and her long blonde hair fell in front of her face. "And what?"

At least she was talking to me, even if it was about things I didn't want to ever talk about. I knew I had to. I couldn't live in denial forever.

"And I was afraid you'd run once you found out," I told her, my biggest fear.

"I can't say what I would have done because you didn't give me the chance."

"Can you really say you would have been okay if I told you I knocked up some girl who I pretended was you? That I gave her money to get an abortion and… and…" I looked up to the sky and yelled. "I thought it was over and done with, but it ate away at me to know I could have had a child, and it was dead." I lowered my head and looked at Lo. "And it wasn't yours."

Her eyes softened in the streetlight for a moment before they hardened. "Nope. We're not talking about this. Good night, Oz."

With those passing words, she walked inside and didn't look back.

THIRTEEN
LO

JANUARY

A SOFT KNOCK on the bedroom door startled me awake. I sat up in bed with my hand over my heart. Charlie flew up to look and then hopped off the bed and sat in front of the door.

I groaned, not wanting to get up. Sliding out of bed, I threw on a sweatshirt over my tank top, unsure of who was at the door, and went to open it. I probably should've asked, but I knew that now that Charlie was up, he would need to go to the bathroom no matter what.

Swinging open the door, West stood there with a leash in hand and a smile on his face. "Sorry, I didn't know you were sleeping, but I thought maybe we could go for a walk and talk."

"Sure," I grumbled. Slipping my feet into a pair of tennis shoes by the door, I took the leash and clipped it onto Charlie's collar. I didn't bother to look at who was sitting in the living room as we passed. Classes hadn't resumed, and the guys didn't have practice, so they'd been camped out in front of the TV for the last week since I'd been back.

I didn't speak until we were out of the house, and I was sure no one would hear me when I spoke. "What did you want to talk about?"

It wasn't normal for West to seek me out, and I had a feeling I wouldn't like how this conversation was going to go down.

"Oz and how depressed he is." He chewed on the inside of his cheek for a moment before he looked at me from the corner of his eye. "I'm worried about him. He's not doing good with you not talking to him. I'm afraid he'll do something stupid while Fin and I are gone."

"Where are you going?" I asked, not wanting to start with the topic of Oz.

"Up to San Francisco for the weekend. It was the… let's just say it's a place that's special for us, and we wanted to get away before school starts again."

"That sounds nice. You know I'm really happy Fin has you. He's…"

"You can say it," he laughed. "Everyone does. He's nicer, but he's still an asshole. He doesn't have to hide a major side of himself from the world. Also, it helps that his dad isn't a part of his life anymore."

"My parents are still talking about how his dad pretty much tried to blackball him with the whole town. I can't believe any parent would do that to their child. I would never do that."

West let out a sad sigh. "Yeah, it's not good, and I'm not sure if he's really dealt with it in all actuality. I think he's happy to no longer feel that pressure he was under and could never live up to. One day it's going to sink in, and then he'll probably be as bad off as Oz is right now."

An angry breath escaped through my nose as I narrowed my eyes at him. "You had to bring it around full circle, didn't you? Having your parent disown you is an entirely different thing than knocking up some girl."

"It is, but Oz doesn't care that some girl is pregnant with his baby. He cares that he's lost you. He's been longing to be with you as more than his sister's best friend for years, and when something finally starts growing between the two of you, this happened. He's lost hope. He's been drinking a lot more than normal, and I'm afraid it's going to become a problem."

I didn't like to think of Oz depressed, but I also didn't

like to think of him with another woman and having a child with her either.

Raising my arms out to my sides, I asked. "How do we go back to what was only just beginning after that?"

"I don't know, but I think it would help if the both of you sat down and talked about what happened. Let Oz tell you his side, and you can tell him how you feel."

"What more is there to say from his side? He had sex with her, and she's pregnant. The. End," I snapped. This was not how I wanted to start my day.

"Yes, there's that, but you have to understand why he didn't tell you. First of all, when you first got here, you were in no condition to hear that, and it wouldn't have made sense for him to tell you. You were friends—barely—even though you both have had feelings for each other for years."

"And look where that got me. The one guy I want, I can't have." I started to walk again.

"Who said you can't have him? He's not with her, and he never intends to be. If you can see past that—"

"That's the problem," I interrupted. "I can't see past it right now. All I can think about is Oz having sex with her, and now she's having his baby."

"I don't know Tori well, but if I were Oz, I would demand a paternity test. What I do know about her is she preys on men when they're drunk and pounces. This child might not even be his."

Stopping in the middle of the street, I turned to look at him. "Do you really believe that?"

"This is Tori we're talking about. She went to Central Valley with me, and she had a bad reputation. I wouldn't be surprised if she took advantage of Oz."

"Yes, I'm sure he was completely unwilling," I muttered and started walking again and away from this conversation.

"I do know he was drunk. Otherwise, he wouldn't have done it. I've heard of Oz's reputation, but I also know he's been trying to fix it in the hopes that one day he'd be worthy of you, and now he sees himself as the lowest of the low."

Shaking my head, I wanted to march back to the house and slap Oz in the face. He never had to do anything to make himself worthy of me.

"Being drunk is a copout. Would you get drunk and fuck someone else?" I spat.

"No, but you also weren't together. There was no relationship even on the horizon between the two of you. I hate to say this, but men have needs, and we're simple creatures. If some girl," he looked at me knowingly. "Shook her ass in front of him when he was drunk and down on himself, well... he was probably picturing you instead of her."

"What good does that do? It doesn't make it like we've actually had sex or that I got pregnant." Even as the words came out of my mouth, I knew they didn't make sense. I huffed. "You know what I mean. It would be different if he was jerking off while thinking about me, but having sex with her and thinking of me is not cool."

"I'm not saying it is, but guys have needs, and he—"

Rounding back on him, my body was shaking. "Don't. I don't want to hear it. What would he think if I was horny, went out and had sex, and then got pregnant? I'm sure he wouldn't see me in the same light."

"I'm sure he'd be plenty upset, but Lo, you're forgetting one thing. While he's loved you for years, you two weren't together. He didn't cheat on you."

"Well, it certainly feels that way," I choked out, tears flooding my eyes.

West walked to me slowly with his arms held out, making sure it was okay before he pulled me into a hug. "I know it does, but you really need to talk to him. We don't want him doing anything else stupid because he's desperate."

No, we didn't, and he was likely to do something dumb.

West pulled back enough to look down at me. "And we still don't know what was going on with him and Dean, but whatever it is, it can't be good."

He was right again. I wondered if Oz would open up to me and tell me what the fight with Dean was about and the night he showed up at our house if I talked to him.

Charlie started pulling me, done with staying in one

place when he wanted to sniff everything around him. West fell into step beside me.

"When we get home, I'll talk to him. It doesn't mean everything is going to go back to the way it was before, though."

West held his hands up. "I know, but I think if you even talk to him, it would do him a world of good." He reached for my hand and gave it a little squeeze before moving away. "Thank you for at least trying with him. I don't know how he's managed to last this week on the couch and not bother you."

Did I tell him how many times I heard Oz come up to the bedroom door and stand out there only to walk away? At least Oz was giving me the space I needed and not pressuring me, but even if I was mad at him, I hated to think Oz was hurting.

A thought came to me. "Did you talk to him like this when I first came here?"

"No," West shook his head. "That was all Oz. He wanted so desperately to take care of you and… to kill the person who hurt you. I think he took all of that rage and used it for good. Now," he shrugged. "I don't know what he'll do with all the bad that's he's been keeping deep down inside."

I moved to walk backward to look at West, but that wasn't a good idea. Charlie thought it was a game and started to run around in circles. I was lucky to keep on my feet until I got him settled down. "Do you really think he's that bad?"

"I wouldn't be out here pushing you to do something you don't want to do if I didn't. Since Tori showed up, he's drinking more than what's healthy. If Coach found out, it wouldn't be good. Off-season or not," he grimaced.

I hadn't thought of that. I knew Oz didn't love the game like West did and wasn't planning on playing in the NFL, but he did love playing with his friends, and I didn't want that taken away from him.

My hand went to the doorknob and was starting to turn it when West stopped me with a hand to my shoulder. "Are you going to be okay talking to him?"

"Yeah, now that I've talked to you, I'm more worried about him than I am mad. At least in this moment. Would you...?" I wasn't sure if I should ask what I was about to ask, but I felt that Oz and I needed some time where the rest of the guys wouldn't overhear us. The house was kind of old, and the walls were thin.

"Would I what? Whatever it is, the answer is yes," he laughed.

"Pfft, what if I was going to ask you if you'd buy me some tampons? I doubt you want to do that."

"Yeah, not really," he scrunched up his nose. "But if you really needed them, I'd make Fin go in and get them."

We both laughed at that. The image of Fin walking out of a drugstore with a box of tampons was hilarious.

"No, really, what were you going to ask?" He finally said once we both calmed down.

Letting Charlie inside, I closed the front door, knowing we'd have an audience if I didn't. "Will you watch Charlie while I go somewhere with Oz to talk?"

"Sure, I'll happily play with the puppy while you go try and make things right with Mr. Downer." He moved by me and held the front door open for me.

"Don't say that," I said quietly, looking toward the window the couch sat under. I didn't want Oz to hear West calling him that. "I'm going to get ready for the day, and then I'll ask him." I narrowed my eyes at him. "Don't mention anything to him."

West's brows shot up. "Why? Are you going to chicken out?"

"No, I just want to mentally prepare myself, and I don't need him all excited before I even say anything to him."

"Fine, fine. Get in there and get ready."

West opened the door, and when I walked inside, all eyes were on me. I gave a slight wave before I headed back to the bathroom to get ready. I wasn't going to do much, but I wanted to brush my teeth and comb my hair. I didn't even know where to go. This town was small with not many options.

Twenty minutes later, I shoved my phone in my purse and walked out of the bedroom. The house was eerily quiet. There was always noise going on with four guys living here, but not now. If they all left, I was going to be pissed. What was the point of West talking to me if he was going to let Oz leave?

The sight of Oz's blond head bent down with his hands on either side of it stopped my movement. How hadn't I noticed how bad off he was? Probably because I had kept to his room for the majority of the time I'd been back. I only came out when I had to; otherwise, I kept my earbuds in and had my music playing around the clock in an effort to not hear what was going on. More like so that I wouldn't hear Oz walk down the hall and then stop outside the bedroom door. I didn't want to be tempted to let him in.

After watching him for several moments, I asked. "Hey, can we talk?"

His head popped up, and his eyes lit up. "Sure. Anything you want."

I gripped onto the strap of my purse. "I was thinking we could go get lunch or something, so we don't have an audience."

One brow rose, but he nodded. "Give me a minute to..." he sniffed his armpit, which made us both recoil. "I'm going to hop in the shower, but I'll be quick."

"Take your time," I told him. I didn't want to be smelling him while I tried to talk to him.

He took off like a bat out of hell and went straight for the shower. The second I heard the water turn on, I sat down on the couch and surveyed all the beer and vodka bottles that were lying around. West was right. Oz really had been drinking a lot more than normal, especially since neither he nor any of the guys drank during the season.

West peeked his head inside from the back door with a hopeful expression on his face. A second later, Fin's popped up above him. It was then that Oz came out of the bathroom. He looked down the hall to where I was sitting and then to the back door with furrowed brows. I gave the guys a thumbs up and then signaled them to shoo. I was pretty sure Oz figured out West had talked to me since we'd left together earlier, but I didn't think it would help if they were spying on what was going on.

Oz's nearly naked body didn't escape my notice. The way the white towel hung low on his trim hips and seemed to emphasize how deep his 'V' went and the treasure trail of hair that led down to the promised land. He was there one second, gone the next, and back out dressed in a pair of gray sweatpants and a white t-shirt a few moments later.

Seriously?

Didn't he know gray sweatpants were like a women's kryptonite? Or maybe he did, and he wore them on purpose.

His hair was still wet, and I watched as a droplet of water dripped from a strand that hung over his forehead. It traveled down his cheek to his neck and then disappeared underneath his shirt.

Oz cleared his throat. "Are you ready?"

"Yeah, do you want to drive?"

Oz nodded slowly. I hated seeing him so sad. Even though I didn't like what he'd done, West was right. Oz didn't cheat on me. Now I just had to hear him out and see if I could forgive him.

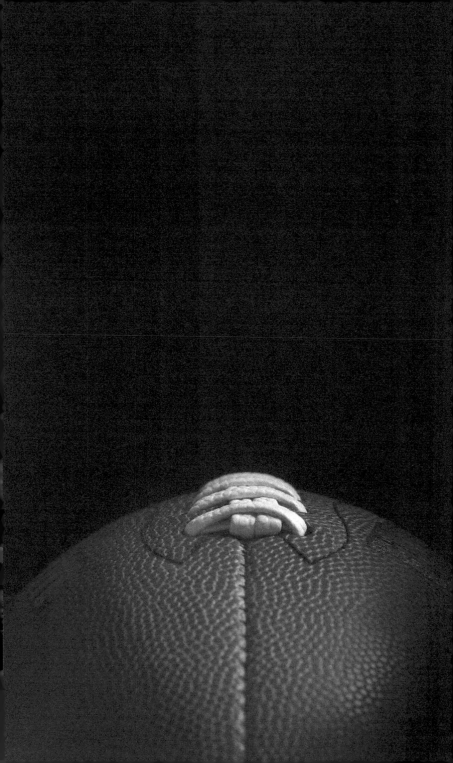

FOURTEEN
OZ

JANUARY

MY BODY BUZZED with Lo in such close proximity. I couldn't believe she was sitting across from me, and we were going to share a meal together. While she had suggested going someplace to eat, she hadn't uttered a word since we left the house.

Instead of waiting for her, I broke the silence. "Not that I'm complaining, but what brought this on?"

She chewed the inside of her cheek for a moment before she braced her hands on the table. "I want to hear your side about what happened with this Tori." Lo spit Tori's name out like it was a curse. Her jealousy was hot.

Fuck. I knew I couldn't lie to Lo, but I also knew she'd be upset with the truth.

"I was stupid first and foremost. In June, when we were back in Santa Lucia, I was out picking up something to eat, and I saw you outside of one of those boutiques you and Dani like to go to."

Lo's brows scrunched together like she was trying to remember where I might have seen her, but she kept silent.

"Anyway, you were talking to some guy. I don't even know who he was. I didn't recognize him, but all I could think about was you hooking up with him. I wanted to stop the thoughts running through my head, so I went to a party Dean was having and got trashed. I don't think I've ever been that drunk in my life."

It was probably because I hadn't consumed any alcohol the entire time I lived in Willow Bay. My tolerance up until recently had been next to nil.

I shook my head, not wanting to say the next part. "I wasn't looking to hook up with anyone. Believe me on that. The place was packed, and Tori sat on my lap, grinding her ass on me while I continued to drink and watched some MMA fight on TV."

Lo's eyes filled with tears, but I knew I had to continue, so we could hopefully move past this.

"I should have knocked her off my lap, but I didn't. I wasn't thinking or feeling or anything," I pursed my lips as I tried to think back that night. It was so hazy. "I don't remember how it happened or even that it did happen. All I know is I woke up in bed the next morning, and she was there next to me."

Luckily, I was interrupted by the waitress bringing us our food. She set our plates down in front of us and gave us an uncomfortable smile. Had she overheard me?

"If you need anything else, let me know," the waitress said as she backed away.

Lo looked at her food and frowned. "Maybe this was a bad idea. My appetite vanished."

I wasn't sure what to say. "I'm sorry. You can take it back home with you if you want, or we can leave."

"No, let's stay. I'll eat some naan at least," she picked up a piece of naan and swirled it through the sauce. "Even though I don't want to hear it, please continue."

"I left when I woke up and didn't look back. Not until Tori told Dean I got her pregnant a couple of months later." I shoved a piece of my chicken tikka masala into my mouth, so I wouldn't have to talk for a minute. I didn't care that I wasn't hungry or that I hadn't been hungry for over a week. I chewed slowly, sucking up every second I could to try and gather myself.

She knew exactly what I was doing. Lo narrowed her eyes as she stared at me from across the table.

I held up my hand. "I met up with Tori, and she showed

me a pregnancy test and said she needed money for an abortion. Which I gave her," I amended. "After that, I never heard from her again until she showed up the day you unexpectedly came home."

"Okay," she nodded. "You never thought about it in all that time?"

"Not really," I shrugged. "Maybe once, but I assumed Tori had the abortion she wanted to get. I mean, I don't even remember being with her, you know?"

"No, I really don't know. Like I told you before, I had only been with one guy before the attack, and I do remember it. Does that happen a lot with you? Not remembering having sex with women?"

"Never. Not once. But when I woke up, my shirt was the only thing I didn't have on. I still had on my tennis shoes and shorts."

Which now made me think.

"My shorts were done up, and I didn't feel any... you know on my dick."

Lo's face went from sad to repulsed. "Any what?"

Fucking hell, she was going to make me say it. "You know, juices. Dried up come."

"Good to know," she said to herself. She ran another piece of naan through her sauce absentmindedly and then looked up. "This is more than I want to know, but do you usually have sex with your clothes on, like your jeans or shorts?"

Yeah, this was more than I wanted to say to her, and what was the point?

"I'm not like I used to be, trying to bag every girl in all of Santa Lucia." I rolled my eyes at the lunacy of the thought. "And that was never the plan, but I've heard the talk. I let my dick rule my life back then, but I haven't been with many people in the last... five years. I was trying to be better, but sometimes I'd fuck up. That being said, back in the day, there were times when I'd just slip my pants down and do the deed."

Lo looked at me with sad eyes, her lips downturned, making me not want to continue.

In for a penny, in for a pound. "But I have to say if I was in a bed, I wouldn't have my pants on."

"Oh, well, that's good to know. It's only when you're what, banging some girl up against a wall that you leave your pants on?"

This was not how I saw our conversation going at all. There were things about my past I didn't want Lo to know about. Hell, I didn't want anyone to know about them if I had a choice.

"I don't want to lie and say it hasn't happened. Like I said, I haven't always been a good guy." Not wanting to see the look on her face, I moved my food around on my plate.

"Oz," she said softly. "You've always been a good guy, even when you were making your way through all the girls in Santa Lucia. Never once did I hear you that you promised them the world. They wanted to sleep with you only so they could say they had sex with you, the hot blond football player. They weren't expecting a relationship out of it."

That was good to know.

Clearing my dry throat that suddenly felt like I'd been walking through the Sahara Desert, I took a sip of water and then asked something I was desperate to know. "And what do you want—or did you want—with me?"

Dropping her food, Lo placed her hands in her lap. "I still want the same things. My feelings for you haven't changed. If that were the case, I wouldn't have been so upset."

I perked up hearing that.

Leaning forward, I stretched my hand out across the table in the hope she would reach out and take mine. "So you're saying you're willing for there to be an us?"

"There can't be any more secrets between us. You know everything about me, and I know there are things you're hiding from the guys and me. I believe that's the reason why you've been saying all those disparaging remarks about yourself these last few months. You think if we find out, you'll lose all of us."

She wasn't wrong. Maybe if I'd kept my mouth shut, she wouldn't have caught on.

"But first, I want to ask you something."

"Anything," I clenched my extended hand into a fist.

"Is it possible you didn't have sex with Tori? From what you've told me, I would think you didn't, except for the fact she said she's pregnant. There's no denying that. I saw how big she was, but is it possible it could be someone else's, and she's using you for money?"

Why hadn't I thought about that? Probably because I felt like this was what I deserved for not waiting for Lo.

"I wouldn't put anything past her, but she's not going to admit it to me." Leaning back in my seat, I took in Lo. She looked good. There was no trace of sadness on her face. In fact, there was a glimmer of hope shining back in her eyes, and her face was tanned for the first time in months.

"You look good," I said before I thought about what I was saying.

"None of that right now." Her mouth turned down. "I'm serious, Oz. What if she's lying to you?"

"I don't know. How do I catch her if she is?" I'd wracked my brain day in and day out trying to remember having sex with Tori, and each time, I came up with nothing.

"Oh my God, you can be so obtuse sometimes," she slapped her hand on the table. "Don't give her any more money and demand a paternity test. See what she does then. If she gets defensive or says no, it probably isn't yours."

Looking up at the ceiling, I confessed something I didn't want to but knew I had to. It seemed to be the running theme of the day. "I don't have any money, to begin with. I've gone through all the money I'll get until the end of summer."

Lo dropped her fork and stared at me. "How much money have you given her?"

Oh, what a tangled web I'd weaved.

"I gave her two thousand dollars when she said she was pregnant and going to get the abortion at the end of the week," I started.

"And, because I know you have more money than that unless your parents are pissed at you. Dani gets—"

"We get the same amount, but my money has been going to other places. I pay for my rent and food here as well."

Lo shook her head. "That still doesn't add up, Oz. What aren't you telling me?"

I clamped my mouth shut, knowing this was it. If Lo learned what I'd done and where my money's been going, she might never want anything to do with me again.

Leaning forward, she gripped my hand and held it between the two of hers. "This is your chance, Oz. I already told you I don't want any secrets between us. If there's any hope of us being together, you'll tell me what else you're hiding." She tilted her head to the side as she looked at me. "Does this have to do with Dean?"

Sometimes I hated how perceptive she was.

Looking out the window, knowing there was no way in hell I was going to be able to tell her with her big blue eyes looking at me, I swallowed down all my fears and started to talk. "Dean's been blackmailing me, so no one finds out. That's where all my money's gone."

"How much have you paid him?" She whispered.

"Too much. The day I had to leave you, and you didn't want me to go, was the last straw. I cut him off. I knew he'd never stop if I kept giving him money every time he spent what I gave him. All in all, it's close to thirty thousand."

"Thirty thousand dollars?" Lo shrieked, gaining the attention of everyone who was in the restaurant with us.

"I know," I turned to look at her and was surprised Lo was still looking at me like I was the same guy I was ten minutes ago. "It's so much, and I told him I couldn't keep paying. My parents would start asking questions."

"Instead, it's me asking all the questions." She leaned forward until she was halfway across the table. "That's a lot of money, Oz. What does he have on you?"

"Tori being pregnant for one. He said he would tell you and Dani if I didn't pay up."

Lo let go of my hand, and I knew this was it. She'd never want anything to do with me ever again. She got up, and my heart dropped, knowing I'd lost her for good. When she moved to sit on my side of the booth and put her arm around me, the world ceased to exist. It was only Lo and me —at least until she spoke. "But there's more, isn't there?"

Resting the side of my head on top of hers, I sighed, defeated. "My senior year in high school, I did something really stupid. I was so lost in wanting you and knowing I'd never get to have you that I made some poor decisions."

She said my name quietly. Her warm breath puffed along the skin of my neck. "That was almost two years ago. You shouldn't have to keep paying for a mistake for that long."

"Well, Dean sees it differently, and I'm sure you will too once you learn what I've done." I sat up in case she wanted to run once she knew.

"Let me be the judge of that." She gripped my shoulder harder, and I wanted nothing more than to tell her everything if it would make Lo Carmichael be my person.

"I was at a party with Dean, of course, and there were drugs there. I don't know what I was thinking, but I smoked some heroin that night."

Lo's head flew up, knocking me in the chin. Her eyes were wide with an emotion I'd never seen on her face before. "What the hell were you thinking?"

"I wasn't thinking. I wanted to forget how I was never going to be with the girl I wanted, no matter how much I wanted to. And you know what?"

She shook her head, her body trembling next to me. "What?" She asked in a barely-there whisper.

"It worked. I forgot about *everything*. I didn't have a care in the world when I was high, and I wanted it again and again. That was until I heard of some guy dying from a heroin overdose. After that, I realized I needed to stop running away from my problems, but Dean didn't like his money train drying up, so he started to blackmail me."

"Oh, Oz," Lo cried, wrapping her arms around me and hugging me fiercely.

To say I was shocked was the understatement of the year. I thought telling Lo my truths would make her run far away instead of bringing us closer together.

"At first, it wasn't money. It was smaller things. Like when we went to Lake Arrowhead, and he came along. Nothing he ever asked for was easy. In fact, each time, it became harder and harder until he wanted money." I closed my eyes, ashamed of all that I'd done to keep Dean quiet. "Please don't tell Fin. If he finds out, he'll more than likely kill Dean and maybe me as well."

Lo shook her head. "Fin won't kill or hurt you. And you can't keep this from him. He needs to know, and if you don't think he's suspicious, you're wrong as hell. I'm sure he's been trying to figure it out since Dean showed up trying to break in that night." Pulling away until her blue eyes were locked on mine, Lo gave me a sad smile. "You should have told him from the beginning. Fin would never have let this go on for so long."

"I couldn't risk him doing something stupid for me. Plus, it's my problem, and I need to pay the consequences."

"No, it's not. Not anymore. From now on, you've got me, and if you want, I'll talk to Fin and tell him what's been going on if you think that will go over better."

"Not happening. I can't have you doing that. I'll tell him… *eventually*," I added with a chuckle.

Lo leaned back and looked up at me with those eyes of hers that were so blue I wanted to drown in them. "When are you supposed to hear from Tori or Dean again?"

And she ruined it.

"With Dean, I never know." I gave her a one-shoulder shrug. "It's pretty much whenever he runs out of money. Since I haven't paid him in a good while, that means he's probably desperate, which isn't a good thing."

Lo hummed. "That means you need to tell Fin and soon."

She was right; I did. It seemed my entire world was going to crumble around me all at once.

"You know what you need to do about him, but what about Tori? When are you supposed to hear from her again?"

"Probably the next time *she* wants money. It seems like that's all everyone wants from me," I sighed.

"Well, the next time she calls, shows up, or whatever she

does, you tell her you're not giving her any money until she has a paternity test. See how easy that was? We solved everything."

For the first time in days, hell months, I felt lighter. With Lo by my side, there was hope for the first time in a long time. And with that hope, I had to ask.

Brushing her hair over her shoulder, I flipped a piece between my fingers. "Does this mean you'll give me a chance?"

Lo smiled coyly at me. "Maybe if you ever ask me out on a date?"

One brow rose as I smiled down at her. "You need me to ask you?" She nodded, and my smile turned into a smirk. "Lo, would you please do me the honor of going out on a date with me?"

Her hand rose to rest on my chest. "Nothing would make me happier. I've only been waiting since the moment I first saw you for you to ask me."

I hummed, putting my hand over hers that still rested on my rapidly beating heart. "It's long overdue for the both of us, isn't it?"

Now I just needed to come up with the perfect date. One we'd both been waiting five years for.

FIFTEEN
LO

END OF JANUARY

I WAS PUTTING on a coat of mascara when Fin leaned against the bathroom doorframe. Not bothering to stop getting ready, I tried to speak with my mouth in an 'O' formation.

"What the hell did you say?" Fin laughed from where he stood.

Putting the wand back inside the tube, I turned to look at him. "Can I help you?"

His brow rose like he didn't believe that's what I'd said. It wasn't, but I thought better of saying something sassy to him when Fin rarely sought me out. "Do you know where you're going or what you're doing?" he finally asked after a moment.

"Not a clue. He's being very tight-lipped about it." I stepped toward him and whispered. "Do you know?"

"Not a clue," he shook his head. "He hasn't said a word, and I'm worried he doesn't know how to plan a proper date." Fin looked down the hall to Oz's bedroom and back to me. "Even if it sucks, act like it's the best damn date you've ever been on."

Putting my hands on my hips, I could feel every bit of my face harden toward him. "I would never make him feel like shit. Now, I can't say the night won't be ruined if Tori magically shows up. Other than that, it's going to be perfect because it's with Oz, and I've been dreaming about this for what feels like forever."

"That's the problem. You both have wanted this for so long that you have these crazy high expectations that likely won't be met. It would kill Oz if he thought he didn't plan the most perfect date ever." Fin leaned forward. "When I tried to talk to him about it, he wouldn't even talk to me about it. He told me to mind my own business. Surely he's come up with something decent in two weeks." He said the last like he didn't believe it.

Both my brows raised, indicating maybe he should have done just that. "What makes you the expert?"

Fin laughed and backed up. "Oh, by all means, I'm no expert, especially where you're concerned. I only want you two to have the best time and for it to be successful. When you learned about Tori being pregnant, it nearly killed him."

"Well, if he would have told us what was going on, it wouldn't have been so bad. It was such a shock, and it happened right when things were changing between us." It nearly killed me.

"Since we're talking about Tori, I think you're right," he whispered. "I don't think he had sex with her. But if the baby is, in fact, his, what's that going to do to the both of you?"

I went back to the sink to finish getting ready. I hadn't given myself the freedom to think about the possibility of Oz fathering that baby. Closing my eyes, I sighed and looked back at him. "I don't know, but I'm not going to pack up and leave. That's all I know."

"Good, because if it is indeed his, Oz is going to need you more than ever. But let's not jump that hurdle until we have to. Do you know if he's talked to her? He's keeping everything close to the vest."

That's because Oz knew once he talked to Fin about Tori, he would to have to tell him about what Dean had on him and that whole ordeal. I hadn't asked questions when he told me about his drug use. I had promised myself I would support him, and I was, but we both knew there would be lots of questions once Fin learned about it. It killed me to know I was the cause of every bad decision Oz made, all because he wanted to be with me, and he felt he couldn't.

It made me wonder how Dani would feel when she found out since she was the one who had kept us apart. She still didn't seem to like the idea, not that there was an us yet. We'd shared one night where we made out and lots of handholding, but that didn't make us a couple.

Would she ever accept us? Maybe if she knew how badly she'd hurt Oz, she'd see things differently. I'm not sure how she couldn't see how much her brother had changed over the years. I'd noticed, but I loved Dani and didn't want to rock the boat. Now, I couldn't help it. I loved Oz more, and if it meant Dani and I weren't as close anymore, then I was ready to make that sacrifice.

"Where'd you go just now?" Fin asked, bringing me out of my reflection.

"Thinking about everything. It's so much, and I'm worried everything is going to come crumbling down. There are so many things pulling Oz in so many directions that I wonder what will happen when it all becomes too much, and he cracks."

One of Fin's brows rose. "Hasn't he already?"

"It could be so much worse," I hinted.

"Do you know *everything*?" Both brows were now up as he looked at me.

"I do, and he's promised he'll talk to you soon. I think he put all his time and energy into this date to avoid talking to you, but he will. Just give him a little more time."

The corners of Fin's mouth turned down. "It's bad, isn't it?"

"Yeah, and he's going to need your help. Please don't judge him too harshly."

Fin scoffed. "As if I'm going to judge him when he fully accepted me being gay. All he wanted was for me to be happy, and I feel the same way about him. I love him like a brother, and I'd do anything for him unless it has to do with West." His eyes changed in that moment, becoming even blacker as he set me in his sights. "Please tell me it has nothing to do with him."

"I can promise you one hundred thousand percent it has nothing to do West or anyone who lives in this house or even in Willow Bay."

"Then I'll tear whoever is apart for doing this to him. Oz is one of the best people I know, and to see what this has done to him pisses me off," he growled.

I knew Fin was serious, and I understood now why Oz was scared to talk to Fin. Fin would want to kill Dean when he learns the truth.

Not wanting anyone to hear what I had to say next, I moved until I was only a few inches away from Fin. "Oz doesn't see himself as that good guy. Not anymore, and we're going to have to help build him back up. I don't understand how this all happened."

"I can't say since I don't know what's going on, but I'll trust you on it." He slapped the door frame, took a step back, and waggled his eyebrows. "Have fun tonight."

I put one final swipe of lip gloss on before I stepped back and looked at myself in the mirror. Usually, I looked more like a tomboy in jeans and t-shirts or like I didn't care in yoga pants. It was a rare occasion when I wore a dress, but I wanted to go all out tonight for Oz. This was our first official date, and I wanted everything to be perfect.

I heard someone walk by, but I was too busy looking at myself in the mirror. What if Oz didn't like how I looked in a dress?

"You look beautiful," West said from the doorway.

"Really? I'm starting to second-guess my choice of outfits. Do you think Oz will like it?" I bit my bottom lip, unsure.

"I'm going to go with 'he's going to be drooling all night' with the way you look, and if he doesn't like it…" West eyes looked me up and down. "Well, he'd be stupid."

"You're just being nice. I don't think he's ever seen me in a dress. I kind of feel exposed." I looked down to the hem of my dress that stopped mid-thigh.

West rolled his lips and did everything in his power to not laugh, but he was wildly unsuccessful.

"What?" I put my hands on my hips, annoyed.

"You say you feel exposed when you walk around here most of the time with fewer clothes on. Which I'm sure Oz very much appreciates."

"Those are my pajamas. I get hot when I sleep, and I can't very well sleep naked now, can I?"

"Why not? We do," Fin yelled from wherever he was in the house.

"TMI," I shouted back.

When I looked back to West, he was shaking with quiet laughter. "Yeah, it's smart to knock before you *ever* come in."

"I'll take that under advisement." I'd never been in their room, and now I definitely wasn't planning on it.

"Keep the dress on. You look beautiful and have fun," West said as he started to leave.

"Wait," I called to him. West peeked back in. "Both you and Fin told me to have fun. Do you really think I won't?"

West cocked his head, his green eyes lit up. "Fin stopped by too?"

"He did, and now I'm starting to get worried." Although I knew whatever Oz planned, I'd love it because I would be spending time with him, and I knew he had tried to make it the best date possible.

"Oh, don't worry. I bet it will be epic, and then Fin will be jealous he never came up with a date that good." He laughed.

"What are you talking about? He just took you to San

Francisco. Are you saying your trip sucked?" I said loud enough for Fin to hear since I knew he was listening.

Not even thirty seconds later, I also had Fin back at the bathroom entrance. "Are you telling her our trip was bad?"

West narrowed his eyes at me, but he had a smile on his face, so I knew he wasn't mad. "I said nothing of the sort. I just said you might be jealous of Oz's date planning, depending on what it is."

"I think you're going to be jealous of Lo if she goes on a good date. Are you saying I need to step up my game?" Fin stared West down. "Maybe you need to step up your game?"

"Okay," I pushed them apart. "I didn't want anything like this to happen. I'm sure you each plan the best dates, and no one needs to one-up the other."

Fin seemed to back down. "I know I'm not some sappy romantic, but don't tell me I suck at planning. I do okay where it matters."

West pulled Fin into a hug and whispered into his ear. When they pulled apart, they kissed. It was brief and kind of hot. They didn't display many acts of affection around the house, but that didn't matter. They always looked at each other with love in their eyes.

"Doesn't Lo look nice?" West indicated to me, and I blushed. I didn't want any more attention, and furthermore, I didn't want to hear Fin tell me I didn't look good.

"Yeah, she looks pretty." He turned to look when West

pointed at me and then rolled his eyes. "*You* look pretty. Perfect for our boy. Now stop stalling. He's in the kitchen probably about to chew one of his fingers to a nub if he waits any longer for you."

"Thank you both. Maybe you two can have a date night while we're gone."

"Oh, I plan on it. Ford is making some new thing that he promises to be orgasmic and then..." Fin waggled his eyebrows.

"Leave the poor girl alone," West slapped him in the stomach. "I think she's nervous."

I was a little, but mostly I was excited. Fin and West were why I started to get nervous, but I shouldn't have let them get to me.

"I'm fine," I said as I pushed between the two of them. The way they ribbed me reminded me of my brother Alex when we were kids.

Slipping inside the bedroom, I grabbed my purse and phone and then headed to the kitchen, where I knew Oz was waiting for me. True to their word, Oz was leaning with his hip against the counter and gnawing on this thumbnail. When he saw me, he stood up and wiped his thumb over his jean-clad legs. I took him in. He wore a dark gray button-down shirt with the sleeves rolled up to his elbows, showcasing the taut muscles in his forearms.

"You look," we both said at the same time and then

laughed. "You go first," Oz gestured to me as he moved closer and took one of my hands in his.

"I was going to say you look good. It's been a long time since I've seen you dressed up." I looked down at what I was wearing and frowned. "I hope this is okay."

Oz shook his head. "It's more than okay. You look absolutely gorgeous. I couldn't ask for a better-looking date."

I could feel my entire body flush at his compliment. "Thank you. Are you going to tell me where we're going yet?" I asked one more time, hoping I'd finally learn where we were going.

"Not yet, but you might want to grab a sweater." He looked down at my feet and then smiled. "And as much as I love seeing you in those sexy heels, you should probably wear some sandals."

"Okay, I'll be right back." I popped up on the tips of my toes and kissed his cheek. "If I forget to tell you later, I had a great time."

Oz laughed, gripping my hips with his large hands and pressing his soft lips to mine. "You can't steal movie lines."

"Even if they accurately depict how I'm feeling?" I asked, backing away.

"Okay, maybe then. Go get your stuff so we can leave, or we're going to be late."

Late to the place where he wouldn't tell me we were going. I had a feeling it was going to be outside, or at least we'd be outside for some of it since he asked me to grab a sweater. Too bad I didn't have one. Instead, I grabbed my sweatshirt, happily removed the heels that were already hurting my feet, and slipped on a pair of sandals.

Oz was waiting for me at the front door when I stepped out. Internally I squealed that I was finally going on a date with him.

Putting his hand to the small of my back, Oz guided us down to his car and even opened up my door for me. Since I knew he wouldn't tell me where we were going, I didn't bother asking again. Instead, I turned in my seat and watched him as he slid inside and then drove us in silence for twenty minutes. His fingertips tapped on the steering wheel the entire time he drove, letting me know he was as nervous as I was, which was sweet. I'd been on dates, and no guy had ever cared nearly as much as Oz did about showing me a good time.

When we pulled up to the bay with the sun setting, I knew tonight was going to be extra special.

I waited as Oz came around and opened my door for me. He wove our fingers together as we walked up to Bay Grill. The place was dimly lit, with each table only lit by candlelight, and the tables were spaced out to give each one privacy. Two walls were floor-to-ceiling windows that showed the bay view with the beautiful setting sun.

"I have a reservation under Francisco," he told the

hostess. She couldn't seem to take eyes off Oz long enough to look to see if we had a reservation or not. While I knew Oz was a damn fine specimen of a man, I would never look at another woman's man the way she was looking at him.

Oz leaned down and whispered in my ear. His lips brushed against the shell of my ear, and his hot breath nearly drove me wild. "If you keep clasping onto my hand that hard, you're going to break it."

He wouldn't let go even as I tried slipping it out as we walked, following the hostess who kept turning to look over her shoulder at us. Was she looking to see if Oz was looking at her ass? When I looked up, Oz was looking down at me with a wry grin on his face. "Don't pay any attention to her. I'm not."

"It's hard when she's been eye-fucking you from the moment we walked inside. Am I invisible to her?"

"You're certainly not to me. In fact, you're all I can see. Do you want me to say something because I will?"

While I did want him to say something, I didn't want to make a spectacle out of myself, all because I didn't like how one person was looking at him. I needed to get used to it if we were going to be together. Otherwise, I was going to walk around like a jealous bitch all the time, trying to claim her territory.

"We have the table you requested ready for you." She

made some stupid showcase move as she indicated a table that was even further away from the others and took center stage in front of the windows. It would give us a perfect view of the sunset and the bay as we ate.

"Thank you," Oz said without looking at her as he pulled out my seat and then pushed it in once I sat.

He sat down across from me and took my hand with his, then rested them in the middle of the table.

"I had no idea this place existed. It has to be hands down the most romantic restaurant ever," I gushed as I looked around. We were so far away from everyone else it was like we were the only two people in the entire restaurant, and we had the sunset and water as our backdrop.

"I'm glad you approve. I haven't been here either, but I did some research on the area, and I heard about this place quite a few times," he flashed me a grin.

"Well, it's perfect. Thank you for taking me here. I can't imagine what you'll do for date two."

His eyes widened in panic. "I hadn't thought of that."

I couldn't help the grin that spread across my face as I spoke. "It's going to be hard to outdo this."

"Yeah, it is," he frowned as he looked around. "Does that mean there will be a second date?"

I shrugged like I didn't know if there would be a second or even a third when I was already picturing us getting married. It would probably be a bad idea to tell Oz I was thinking about what our kids' names would be.

"Do you want kids?" I rushed out.

Oz cocked his head to the side, and a smug grin stretched across his face. "Is that some sort of criteria for a second date?"

"Maybe," I retorted. If Oz never wanted children, then maybe he wasn't the man for me.

"I don't want kids *now,* and definitely not with anyone but you. In eight to ten years, maybe we could start. I want to have years of you all to myself, and once we're successful and traveled the world, *then* we can have kids."

Damn, that was one smooth answer.

"What else do you see in our future?" I wanted to hear more about what else he saw for our future.

"Hmm, I don't know where we'll live just yet, and I don't care where we end up as long as we're happy. Hopefully, our jobs will afford us time to travel. Maybe we can even vacation with Fin and West," he smiled shyly, and it was so sweet. It made me want to lean across the table and kiss him. "When we feel the time is right, we'll start a family."

"I like that," I quietly said. "Do you really think Fin and West will stay together?"

"I sure as fuck hope so. I can't imagine what Fin would do or who else he'd be with. He'd be a sad son-of-bitch that I wouldn't want to deal with."

I didn't want asshole Fin back, making me hope they stayed together forever as well.

"I like them together," I told him. "But let's get back to future *us*."

He reached his hand out across the table. I wasted no time lacing our fingers together. "What more would you like to hear?"

"Are we getting married sometime before we have kids, or are we living in sin for the rest of our lives?"

A wicked grin turned the corners of his mouth up. It had been a long time since I saw Oz smile so much. "We haven't sinned *yet*."

The operative word was *yet*. Oz had already put the brakes on once, and I wondered how long it would take him to realize I was ready for him. With the help of my therapist, I had healed emotionally, and physically I'd mended long before that. With Oz finally opening up to me about all of his secrets, we were connected more now than ever.

"Maybe we should look at the menu, so we can continue our night," he lifted his menu, making me do the same. I looked for a moment, and when I saw fried shrimp, I knew that's what I wanted. The moment I looked up, Oz waved over a waiter.

He was young, around our age, and smiled shyly at us. "Have you decided?"

Oz nodded his head toward me. "What would you like, Lo?"

"I'll have the jumbo fried shrimp with a loaded baked potato and seasonal vegetables. Can I get a sweet tea as well?"

"Of course, anything you want," the waiter replied, turning to Oz. "And for you, sir?"

"I'll have the filet mignon, medium, with a loaded baked potato. I'll just continue having water," Oz smiled over at me, dismissing our waiter.

"Very well, I'll bring your tea after I put in your order." The waiter retreated, and we were once again alone.

"Do you think they'd be mad if we moved our chairs so that we're both facing the window?"

Oz scoffed. "Who cares? We're paying customers. Let's make the most out of our night." Oz stood, and I went along with him. He moved our chairs until they were side by side, facing the window.

The sun sat low in the sky, turning a beautiful pinky-orange, with cloudy white wisps decorating the sky.

"This is nice. I haven't been to the bay since I've been here. In all actuality, I haven't been to many places, but I want to change that. I want to get to know Willow Bay since it's going to be my home."

Oz smiled at me. "I like you calling Willow Bay home. Do you plan to go to classes next fall?"

"That's the plan. I thought about asking if I could opt to have some online classes, but I don't think it's possible. Well, it is, but since I'm switching my degree and the classes will be harder, I'll need to be in class in case I have any questions or need the help of study groups. Classes are boring, though. Maybe we can go to a couple of Dani's games."

Oz's eyes lit up at the mention of his sister. I loved how close they were. Sometimes it made me wish I was that close to Alexander. "She'd like that. I wish she played here so it would be easier to see her play. We hardly ever get to go to each other's games, and I miss watching her. If she keeps up playing the way she has, she'll be in the running for the Olympics." He beamed. "To think that my baby sister could be in the Olympics someday is astonishing."

It really was. Dani had trained so damn hard. Just as hard as the guys.

Because of our easy conversation, our food was placed in front of us in what seemed like only minutes later, making my mouth water. For a few moments, we ate in silence, enjoying our food with little smiles and moans. Maybe that was just me, but the food was damn good. Not as good as the food Ford cooked for us on a daily basis. Well, he made me the best food while he usually made the guys their boring, healthy food.

It was Oz who broke the silence. "I thought when we're

done eating, we could take a walk on the beach. Maybe we can get dessert to go."

"Is there a make-out session on the agenda?" It had been two weeks since our lunch, but I'd forgiven Oz. Things didn't go back to normal right away, but they were getting there. Oz still slept on the couch no matter how many times I told him now that school was back in, he needed to get a good night's sleep. He resisted, but I hoped tonight would be a turning point. I missed him. My anger had faded into worry. I hadn't realized how much Oz had been internalizing, and I hated he'd kept everything to himself—that he felt the need to. Now, if he would only tell Fin about Dean, we could figure a way out of that mess.

Oz brought our hands up to his mouth and kissed the back of my hand. "Wipe that worry off your face. Tonight is for us. Tomorrow we can work to figure out everything else. Are you ready to get out of here?"

I nodded, wanting nothing more. We needed a place where it was just us. Oz stood and threw a few bills on the table. He held out his hand, helping me up and pulling me into a hug. I loved the way it felt to be in his arms. I never wanted to be anywhere else.

Instead of going out the front door, we went out to the deck and took the stairs down to the beach. Now it made sense why Oz wanted me to wear sandals. If I had worn heels, the beach would've been ruined. We both took off our shoes and placed them by the stairs.

Lacing our fingers together, Oz led us down to the water, and we walked along just outside the reach of the water.

"How do you know me so well?" I laughed. It was like he could read my mind sometimes. He always knew what I needed.

"Maybe I shouldn't tell you. I'll probably sound like a stalker, and then you'll want to run away." He said the words like a joke, but I knew he was serious.

"You're not getting rid of me that easily," I told him, hoping to release him from his fears. "If you don't think I've watched you at every opportunity, you're wrong. I know you, Oz, just as you know me. The only thing I wish is that we would have started this back in high school." We'd lost so much time, but not any longer. Tonight was the start of our lives together.

"I agree, but we both know why we waited." I nodded because I did. I didn't want to lose my best friend, and he didn't want to lose his sister. "Hopefully, when Dani realizes I won't hurt you, she'll be happy to see us together. I don't want it to be uncomfortable every time we see her."

"I know. Me neither, but she's open to it. Maybe it has something to do with her finally having a boyfriend."

Oz grumbled under his breath. "Don't remind me. I'm not sure I like that guy."

"Me neither. Declan was… intense, but I'm willing to give him the benefit of the doubt if she does the same for us."

"I like it when you say *us*." The way he said us made butterflies flutter in my stomach. Did he feel the same way when I said it?

"I'm not sure I can keep walking on this beach with you looking at me like that," he growled.

"Like what?" I asked, curious.

"Like you love me," he said, barely more than a whisper over the sound of the water.

"I do love you, Oz." I stopped and cupped his cheek with my hand. "How can you not know that?"

He tried to look away, but I held him in place. "I don't deserve you. I've done nothing for you to love me."

"And yet, I do. Nothing you say is going to stop me. You've been with me night after night, slaying my demons each time they invaded the darkness. You gave up your bed for months and spent every last second of your free time with me when you could have been out doing things that were more fun than taking care of a scared girl."

He leaned into my hand. "I didn't want to be anywhere else but with you. You being here was never a hardship. I did it because I love you."

A bubble of laughter gurgled up inside of me, and I clapped my hand over my mouth.

Oz's brows furrowed. "Why are you laughing?"

I clutched the hand I was still holding tighter. "Did you ever think we'd profess our love for each other on our first date?"

"Well, seeing as I never thought we'd have a first date, no," he laughed along with me. "But since we seem to be doing this whole thing ass-backward, I think it's fitting."

"You're right. The only way it could have been more backward is if we were married first," I giggled.

He cleared his throat. "Don't think for one moment I wouldn't marry you because I would in a heartbeat, but I think we should wait until after we graduate."

"Did you just propose to me?" This had to be the strangest and best first date ever.

Oz shook his head. "Not yet. It doesn't count until I have a ring."

Leaning forward, I rested my forehead on his chin. "It could count if you want it to."

Oz brushed his lips to mine before he leaned down and brought our foreheads together. "While you seem eager to say yes, that was not a proposal." His forehead rolled against mine.

Running my fingers through his hair at the nape of his neck, I asked. "Can I say something?"

He closed his eyes and nodded. "You can say anything, anytime."

This felt so right. Oz was happy, and I felt better than ever.

"This is the best date ever."

Oz's eyes popped open. His blue gaze burning. "I'm glad we did this."

"Me too, but I still don't know how you're going to beat this."

But I couldn't wait to find out.

SIXTEEN
OZ

FEBRUARY

MY BACK WAS to the headboard when Lo rolled over with a sleepy smile on her face. Her arm snaked around my waist as she looked up at me. It didn't take her long to notice something was up with me. She sat up and took my hand in hers, bringing it to her chest, where she clutched it.

She took in every detail of my face, and with each passing inch, her forehead puckered a little bit more. "What's wrong?"

Tilting my head up to look at the ceiling, I confessed what I was about to do. "Today, I'm telling Fin about Dean."

Her grip on my hand tightened. "Did he contact you again?"

"Not yet, but I know it's only a matter of time before he either calls or shows up, and I want to be ready. Plus, I don't want any secrets between any of us."

The bed jostled, and a few seconds later, Lo was curled up on my lap with her arms around me. I held onto her tight, letting her anchor me to what was important.

"I know it's going to be hard, but you'll feel so much better once it's all out in the open," she said, her breath fanning out on my neck.

She was right; only I wasn't sure Fin would be as forgiving as Lo. Her faith in me astounded me at every turn. I didn't deserve this woman, but I wasn't going to let her go, either. She was my everything.

"When do you want to do it?"

"The sooner, the better. The longer I think about it, the sicker I get. The thought that I'm about to ruin his weekend…" My stomach rolled just thinking about it.

She pulled away to straddle me. Cupping my cheeks in her small hands, Lo pressed kisses all over my face before she sat back. "You won't be ruining anything. In fact, I'm sure he'll be relieved to finally know the truth. He's probably been racking his brain trying to figure out what Dean has on you."

I groaned and sat Lo on the bed. "I'm ready."

She nodded with a bright smile. If she believed in me,

I could do this. "Why don't I make us all some toast and scrambled eggs, and we can eat breakfast and talk about it."

Taking a deep breath, I left my bedroom and headed to Fin's room. Their door was closed, and I hoped they weren't asleep. I needed to do this now. I gave the door two short raps before I opened it up to find Fin lying in bed with his head thrown back in ecstasy.

Covering my eyes, I turned away from the door. "Oh my God, I'm sorry. When you two get done, can you meet me in the kitchen?"

"Get the fuck out," Fin yelled as I closed the door.

I ran down the hallway and to the kitchen, trying not to laugh. I couldn't believe I just walked in on that.

Lo was at the stove sprinkling cheese into the eggs. "What was all that?"

"You don't want to know. I walked in on something," I laughed, shaking my head.

Her eyes went wide. "Really?" She asked excitedly.

My brows puckered. "Why are you so excited about that?"

She grinned and leaned toward me, whispering. "Do you think he'll want to kill you?"

"Maybe if I saw West, but it was all Fin. Plus, I've seen all the guys naked before in the locker room. It's not something I haven't seen before."

"Yeah, but you haven't seen *that*." She waggled her eyebrows.

"No, that was the first and last time for me. If I made a habit of walking in on them, Fin would probably kill me." Speak of the devil. The sound of heavy footsteps coming down the hall filled the air, making me step closer to Lo.

Fin's eyes narrowed on me. "This better be good. I could barely finish."

I rolled my eyes at him. It had been nine months since I had sex, and it had only been me and my hand since then.

"Sit," Lo called from the stove. "I'm making scrambled eggs and toast."

Fin arched back, looking down the hall. "Where's Ford? Shouldn't he be cooking for us?"

"For now, I just want it to be us," I sat down at the table and crossed my arms over my chest. "I wanted to tell you about Dean and what he has on me."

"Can West be here? You know that unless you tell me not to say something to him, I will."

"I know, and I assumed he'd join." While I liked Ford, I wanted to see what Fin had to say first. I'd tell him Dean was a problem and let him know what's going on from here on out.

Fin let out an ear-piercing whistle that had me close to smacking him upside the head. Luckily West did it for me, but then he planted a kiss on Fin's cheek before he sat down.

"What's going on?" West's green eyes bounced from person to person.

"Our boy here has finally come to his senses and is going to tell us what he's been hiding," Fin's eyes stayed on me the entire time he spoke.

Lo had perfect timing as she set down a plate in front of both Fin and West and then brought over our plates. She sat down beside me and then placed her hand on my bouncing knee under the table.

For the next half hour, I went through everything that had happened with Dean, starting with the first time I did heroin, up until he showed up at the house. Once I was done, both West and Fin sat back in their seats and stared at me.

Fin scrubbed a hand down his face and looked at me with a world of sadness reflecting back. "How the hell did I not see this?"

"Because I didn't want you to. The drugs were short-lived. It's Dean who's been the constant. At first, I paid him because I felt guilty. I was stupid to ever think I could forget about the way I feel about Lo." I looked over at her with a sad smile. Maybe if I had stood up to Dani, none of this would have happened.

Fin leaned his elbows on the table as his eyes bored into mine. "Do you know how lucky you are that you're not some drug addict or that you didn't kill yourself or someone else?"

"I do. I was so fucking stupid, and I knew I should've told you the first time Dean came to me for money. Now, I don't know what to do. It's been too long since I've heard from him, and I know he's getting desperate if I'm the one supporting his drug habit."

Lo leaned into me. Her hand ran up the center of my back and tangled her fingers in my hair. "Now we need to come up with a plan, so we'll be prepared. I don't want us to be desperate when he shows up unexpectedly."

"We won't be, and you're not giving him another dime, do you hear me?" Fin landed a stare on me that I'd only seen him give other people—the one that scared every person he gave it to and usually had them pissing themselves. He was dead serious, and I wasn't going to fuck this up. I needed their help for Dean's bullshit.

Lo leaned forward, eyes bouncing back and forth between us all. "So, what's the plan?"

West shook his head and looked at my best friend. While Fin wasn't evil, he could come up with some awful shit. "This isn't my area of expertise."

"I don't know," Fin exclaimed, exasperated. "It's not like we can kill him and get away with it. I'm assuming no one else knows about this?"

I shook my head. "No one, unless he told Tori, which I could see him doing. She's never mentioned it, and she had the perfect opportunity to do so when she was here demanding money."

"Who do these assholes think you are? Do they not realize you're on a set income until you turn twenty-five?" Fin growled.

"Obviously not. I don't spend all the money I get, but they've—well, mostly Dean—has run through all of what I'd saved. I've got next to nothing until the end of summer. I can't give him another ten thousand dollars," I hung my head. I couldn't believe this was where I was all because of one stupid mistake. If I'd never given in to Dean that first time, none of this would have happened.

As if Lo could read my thoughts, she wrapped her arm around my shoulders and leaned against me. "We're going to figure this out. Don't worry."

"How can I not worry?" My head shot up, and I looked at everyone around the table with me. "I have two people who are trying to ruin my life, and they're doing a pretty damn good job of it. We can't kill Dean, and I have no money to give him. What are my options?"

We all sat in silence after that. I was afraid it was because they realized I had no options. I was screwed.

"Do you have anything you can use against him?" West asked, bringing us all out of our internal musings.

"Not really," I wished I had. "I think most people know by now he's a dealer and uses."

"We didn't." Fin gave me a knowing stare, making me feel even worse for keeping this from him for so long. "So, there could be others he doesn't want to know his business." Fin's black eyes lit with vengeance. "You could go to the cops. Work with them to bring Dean down. I'm sure the police in Santa Lucia would like nothing more than to take down a drug dealer in their own backyard."

West and Lo nodded along with every word Fin was saying. He was right. The only way to take him down was with police involvement. Still, the thought made me uneasy.

Placing his hand on my arm, Fin leaned forward as if whatever he was going to tell me was important. "You're not going to get in trouble. What are they going to say? Oh, you did this drug two years ago. We have no proof, but we're still going to arrest you?" Fin paused with a tilt of his head. "It was just back in our senior year in high school, right?"

Internally I rolled my eyes, but I deserved this line of questioning. They were taking this way better than I thought they would, so I should be thanking my lucky stars that they weren't all furious at me and my stupidity.

"Yes, it was only a few times. It was something I wish I'd never done. I can't promise to always be perfect, but I won't ever do anything like that again."

Fin's nostrils flared. "I fucking hope not. If you do, I'll kick your ass from here all the way back to Santa Lucia, and then I probably will kill Dean."

He made it sound like I was a drug addict.

West's face softened as he leaned forward. "You're so very lucky. You know that, right? You can get addicted to heroin the first time you use it. If that happened, where would you be now?" His eyes darted to Lo, and my stomach sank.

There was no chance in hell Lo would be sitting by my side if I were a drug addict.

"I would have lost everything, and I know that." I hung my head, closing my eyes so tight, stars appeared in my vision. "You have no idea how much it means to me that you're not railing on me or that you want to have anything to do with me after what I told you."

Fin's black eyes drilled into me. "You are like a brother to me. There's nothing you could do that would ever make me give up on you."

And I knew that deep down. Fin hadn't had an easy life with his father, always making him feel less than, only to disown him once he found out Fin was gay. In a way, I think it freed Fin to be who he really was, but deep down, I knew it had to hurt to have your parents give up on you.

"I love you too," I chuckled, which in turn had Fin's eyes narrowing.

"And what's funny about that?" Fin gritted out.

"Not a damn thing, but I was thinking about the day we met. Never would I have thought we'd be where we are now."

"We're friends for life. This isn't going to end once we

graduate. I'm going to be the best man at your wedding when you finally get off your ass and make things official with her." Fin nodded to Lo.

I looked to Lo to find her blushing up a storm, but the way she looked at me made me catch my breath. The love I saw reflected back astonished me.

"Oh, we're official but not quite ready for marriage." I leaned down and kissed her on the temple. "Let me assure you, though. I will marry her one day in the not-too-distant future."

Ford sleepily walked in and then took a step back when he saw us all sitting around the table. "Who cooked?"

Lo raised her hand. "That would be me. We were hungry, and I didn't want to wake you."

Ford looked to Fin and then West. Fin scooted his chair back and stood. "I'm not kicking you out because you didn't cook one goddamn meal. I'm going to take a shower." He looked pointedly down at West.

A shy smile crept along West's mouth. "A shower sounds nice."

Lo jumped up from the table and put her hand on my shoulder. "And that's our cue to take Charlie for a walk."

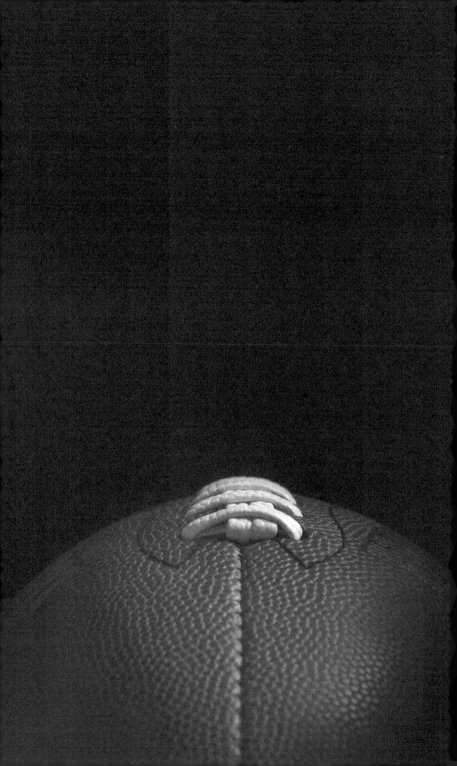

VALENTINE'S DAY

"SO, where is my brother taking you?" Dani asked as she curled her hair via FaceTime.

"Your guess is as good as mine. He insisted on it being a secret." I hesitated to say the next part, but I wanted Dani to be a part of every aspect of my life. "And to pack a bag for the weekend."

Her blue eyes widened comically. "Have you two…"

"Not yet," I shook my head. "He hasn't thought I was ready and wants to make the first time special."

"Ah, who knew my brother is such a romantic?"

I did. In fact, everything Oz did with me was special.

"I'm kind of nervous, and not because I'm not ready, but because…" I didn't want to say why. It was embarrassing, and it would remind her of why she didn't want me with her brother.

She put down her curling iron and picked up her phone before she sat down on her bed. "Talk to me. You can tell me anything."

I moved further out into the backyard and threw the ball for Charlie. "I'm not experienced, and—"

"And Oz has been with every woman under the sun," she interrupted.

"A bit of an overstatement, but yeah, he has. What if he's disappointed in me?" I confessed.

"Oh, honey," Dani's eyes softened. "As much as I didn't want this to happen, I know my brother loves you, and there's nothing you could do to make that change."

"I hope so," I murmured. As if he knew we were talking about him, Oz showed up at the back door of the house and looked out at me. I was sure he was wondering why I wasn't getting ready. I held up a finger and turned my back to him. "Hey, Dani, I need to go, but thanks for talking me out of my freak-out." I was still nervous, but I knew Oz loved me, and we would figure everything else out. "I hope you have a romantic night with your guy."

She rolled her eyes but smiled. "I'd be happy if we spent the night in bed, but he insisted we do the whole shebang."

"You deserve to have a special night." Maybe he wasn't so bad after all. Dani sure seemed to like him.

"And so do you. Now go, so my brother doesn't call me, telling me I'm fucking up his perfect night," she laughed.

I laughed but then sobered. "Hey, Dani, thanks for accepting this. It means a lot to both of us."

"You have to know I'd do anything for you, and if that means dating my brother, then so be it. But he better never hurt you, or I'm going to chop off his nuts."

I looked back over my shoulder to find Oz gone. "He won't. I believe in him."

"Good. Call me when your weekend's over, so we can compare our Valentine dates."

"Will do. Love you," I told her as I tapped the side of my leg to get Charlie to fall in line with me.

"Love you too, girl," she said with a bright smile.

Stepping inside, I found West and Fin coming out of their bedroom with bags over their shoulders. "Where are you two going?"

Fin stopped, blocking the hall. "Did you think only Oz could come up with a romantic night?"

West put his arm around Fin's waist and guided him the rest of the way down the hall. "Don't listen to him."

"Hey, Fin," I called to him and waited until he turned around to look at me. His black eyes met mine, and even though he tried to hide it, I could see this really bothered him. "I know whatever you planned will be perfect for the two of you." I wanted to say I could tell he loved West very much, but I held back.

He nodded but didn't say more.

"Where are you going?" I asked, curious.

"Lake Arrowhead," West beamed.

"Isn't that where you were snowed in together?" I asked, remembering our trip there and Fin being gone one night. After he returned home, he was an even bigger asshole than normal.

"We're going to stay at the resort I worked for and do some skiing," West looked at Fin dreamily.

Fin leaned over and whispered in West's ear, but not quietly enough. I heard every word. "And maybe recreate our first time together."

"Okay," I pushed by them. "I'm going to finish getting ready. Have a great time."

"You too," West replied.

Opening the bedroom door, I found Oz sitting on the bed with his knees bouncing. I sat down beside him and put my hand on one of his knees. "Are you okay?"

"Yeah," he looked at me with a lopsided smile. "I'm anxious to get on the road."

"And yet you still won't tell me where we're going?" Why did he insist on surprising me all the time?

"It wouldn't be a surprise then, wouldn't it?" He laughed. "I did pack your suitcase with the help of Dani."

How had she conspired with Oz and not even mentioned it?

The corners of my lips tipped down. "Strange, Dani told me to tell you hi."

"Hey," he put his arm around me. "I wanted to make sure you'd have what you need. If you don't like what I packed, I'll buy you new clothes, and I'll never surprise you again."

Now was probably a bad time to remind Oz he didn't have money to waste on things like clothes because he wouldn't let me pack. I could provide for myself.

"I need about ten minutes, and then I'll be ready to go. How should I dress?"

Oz looked me over from head to toe. "You can wear what you have on since we'll be in the car for a while. and then you can change or whatever when we get to... where we're going."

Damn, for a second there, I thought he was going to slip and give something away.

It didn't take me long to swipe on a coat of mascara and some lip gloss. I grabbed a sweatshirt since I didn't want to be cold in the car and headed into the living room, where both Oz and Ford were standing by the door. Charlie sat between the two with his head up, looking up at them like their pockets were full of treats just for him.

"What are you going to do since you have the whole place to yourself?" Oz slapped Ford on the back and gave him a sly grin.

"Nothing much since I don't have a girl. I'll probably call my mom and see how she's doing. My sister said she's been acting strange, and I want to check in on her. I'll probably take Charlie on a few walks and see if I can pick up a girl." Ford rubbed Charlie behind the ears, which made Charlie wag his tail happily.

I wasn't sure how I felt about Ford using my dog as a chick magnet, but it was sweet of him to offer to watch Charlie while we were gone for the weekend.

"There's a list on the fridge in case—"

"I know, and we'll be fine. You don't need to worry." Ford interrupted and then looked to Oz. "Can you imagine what she's going to be like when she's a mother?"

Pulling me closer, Oz kissed the top of my head. "The best damn mom ever."

"I hope your mom's okay," I told him. Ford was so sweet to be worried about his mom.

"Well, we're out of here. Don't have too much fun here without all of us," Oz waved to Ford as he guided me out the front door.

A COUPLE OF HOURS LATER, Oz pulled up to a cabin that was in some remote area. I had no idea where we were, but it was beautiful. The cabin was surrounded by trees that looked as if they could touch the sky, and that sky was the bluest of blues I'd ever seen. Behind the cabin, you could see a dock that led to a pristine lake.

The moment Oz turned off the car, I launched myself at him.

"Oh my God, Oz, this place is beautiful. How did you find it?" I asked as I placed kisses all over his smiling, happy face.

He laughed, pulling me tighter against him. "I have my ways. Are you ready to see the inside?"

I hated to ask, but I had to. "How did you afford this?" When his sad eyes looked up at me, I realized how my words sounded. Harsh. "I love it, and I'm appreciative, but I hope you didn't…" I wasn't sure how to make it sound better.

"Don't worry; I didn't bankrupt myself." His hand slid up my back. "But I totally would have for our first Valentine's Day together."

Leaning down, I pressed my lips to his. When his tongue swept along my bottom lip, I opened up to him, ready for more. So much more.

It wasn't long before Oz pulled back with a sexy grin on

his face. "Let's take this inside. We've got the whole weekend to enjoy each other without anyone else around."

While I loved living in a house full of guys, there was no privacy most of the time.

I climbed off his lap and back into my seat, eager to get our weekend started. Before I could open my door, Oz was there holding it open with his hand out for me to take. Slipping my hand into his, I let him help me out of the car.

For a moment, we stood looking up at the cabin. I was in awe at what Oz had come up with. He was perhaps the best man in the world at planning dates.

"You're a true romantic." I curled myself around his arm. "Even in my fantasies, I never would have dreamed up this place, and it's perfect. The only thing that would make it better is if it snowed."

Kissing the top of my head, he held me tighter. "I can't promise you snow, but I can promise you everything else."

"See? Romantic." Tilting my head up, I kissed the underside of his chin.

"Well, if that's the case, then let me woo you the best that I can." He said as he guided me up the path and to the front door. I couldn't believe we were finally here. Tonight would change everything between us.

The second we stepped inside, my breath caught. Rose petals trailed a path between a rustic living area and the kitchen and up the stairs.

"How did you do this?" I tried to take it all in as Oz led us over to a fireplace that I hadn't noticed was lit.

"I can't have you knowing all my secrets, now can I?" He laughed as he pulled me down on a plush, white fur rug that sat in front of the fire. It was welcoming and toasty as I settled between his legs.

"This is already perfect, and I'll probably never want to leave. Do you think the owner will let us buy it?" I joked. I wanted to ingrain this weekend into my memory to keep for the rest of my life.

"I like the way you're thinking, but I'm not sure I want to live somewhere so remote *all* the time. Maybe we can use it as a vacation home. Someday," he added, pulling my back flush against his front.

It felt strange but nice to think of a future with Oz. I knew if this didn't work out between us, we'd both be heartbroken.

Leaning around, he looked at me with furrowed brows. "What are you thinking so hard about?"

"Stupid stuff," I sighed. "Like how much it would suck if we don't work out. One minute, I'm planning our future, and the next, I think about what if we never get that future."

Gripping my hips, he turned me until I was straddling him. His face turned from worried to fiercely determined in two seconds flat. "That's never going to happen. I'm not letting anything or anyone ever take you away from me."

Cupping his face with both of my hands, I looked down at him. My golden god, with his intense blue eyes, stared back at me. "I won't let anyone take you away from me either." I brushed my lips to his, only to pull back and say, "I love you."

Oz claimed me in a kiss that was far from the sweet kisses I was used to receiving from him. Tonight, he was claiming me. Making me his in a way I'd never been.

"I want you," I moaned against his mouth, my core rubbing against the steel erection tenting his pants. "Please," I begged. I needed more. So much more than the over-the-clothes action I'd been getting for the last month.

Standing with me, Oz's hands slid down to my ass and held me there as he started for the stairs. "I wanted to wine and dine you before I took you upstairs, but I can't deny you. Not now. Not ever."

Butterflies took flight in my stomach and made loop de loops with each step he took closer to our destination. I kissed along his jawline, up his neck, and nipped at his earlobe, needing to show him how much I wanted him and this.

The second he set me down on my feet, my hands were busy with the buckle of his belt and swiftly unzipped his jeans. I palmed his erection through his underwear, making him jerk under my touch, and a moan escaped from his soft lips.

"Fucking hell, Lo, you're going to unman me before I get the chance to see you naked," he groaned, stepping back. "Let me undress you and see every inch of your beautiful body."

I wanted nothing more. He was lucky I didn't rip both our clothes off. Maybe he'd been trying to drive me crazy with want this whole month on purpose because in that moment, I wasn't thinking about how I wouldn't be enough for him or that I wouldn't be what he wanted in bed. There was still a little place in the back of my mind where I worried I might freak out even though I knew I was safe with Oz. My rape had irrevocably changed me, and I hoped it didn't prove me incapable of having sex with the one person I had always wished was my first. I wanted this connection with Oz.

I nodded, eager for him to see me because I was desperate to see all of him. While I'd seen Oz in various stages of undress, the thought of seeing all of him had my mouth watering.

"I need you naked too," I said as he reached for the hem of my shirt and started to pull it up and over my head.

"Patience. You'll be lucky if we put on any clothes between now and the time we leave." His deft hands went to the clasp on my bra and had it off in record time. Kneeling before me, Oz gripped the waistband of my yoga pants and started to pull down. "Fucking hell, Lo. Give a guy some warning. I didn't know I was going to come face to face with your perfect pussy this fast."

He pulled my pants down to my ankles before leaning forward and running his nose across my nub. "You smell like heaven," he moaned. "I'm going to worship you the way I've dreamed."

"Yes, please." I wanted to feel his mouth between my legs almost as much as I wanted to have him sink deep inside of me.

Picking me up behind the knees, Oz placed me on the bed and ripped my leggings off the rest of the way, leaving me bare before him.

His big hands ran up the inside of my legs and pushed my thighs open wider as he took me in. "Did you do this for me?"

I nodded, blushing at my daring act of shaving myself and leaving no chance of hiding.

Using his thumbs, he spread me wide as his head bent down, and he licked a slow path up my slit. My hips jerked up off the bed at the exquisite pleasure his tongue brought me. I had no idea it could feel this way. Placing my legs over his shoulders, Oz's hands went to my hips and held me in place as he continued to make leisurely licks like he was eating an ice cream cone.

I moaned and arched into his touch, needing more. "More," I pleaded.

Oz's head shot up, and he licked his glistening lips. His thumb slowly circled my clit as he stared down at my bare core. I wanted to close my legs and hide, but the hungry look in his eyes stopped me.

"You've got the prettiest pussy I've ever seen. I've been dreaming of this moment for..." his eyes came up and met mine. "For years. You're so fucking beautiful, Lo. My dream come true."

"You're mine. I want to see you naked and be able to touch you." I reached for his shirt at the nape of his neck and pulled, giving me what I wanted, or at least some of it. It seemed Oz liked to torture me.

He removed his shirt before lifting my hips off the bed and burying his face between my legs again. Leaning up on my elbows, I watched as he devoured me like I was his breakfast, lunch, and dinner. I never wanted him to leave if it always felt this good. His warm and wet tongue plunged inside of me while he circled my clit with his thumb until my entire body was coursing with unbridled pleasure.

Switching it up, two fingers pumped in and out of my slick core as his soft tongue swirled around my throbbing clit. My back arched as euphoria took over my body. I was no longer Lo Carmichael. There was only the way my body shook and craved for more with each passing touch.

One second I was floating on cloud nine, and the next, I

was slowly starting to come back down to earth. Oz's movements slowed as my body relaxed into the bed.

Even spent, I wanted more. I wasn't sure if I was ever going to want to stop, and I knew the night was only going to get better.

I pulled on his hair until his blue eyes met mine. "Come up here, but first, take off the rest of your clothes," I demanded.

A slow, sexy smirk crossed his face as Oz stood and quickly removed his pants and boxer briefs. My gaze stayed transfixed on what I wanted to see most. I wasn't sure what I thought Oz's cock would look like, but I didn't expect it to be as long and thick as it was with a pink tip that glistened.

Oz climbed up on the bed, dragging me until I was draped on top of him. Propping my chin on my arm, I looked up at him. He had his eyes closed and a dreamy expression on his face. With the way he was looking, it was like he just experienced the best orgasm of his life.

"That was… wow. I've never had that done before." It was slightly embarrassing, but what did it matter. If I could have, I would have had Oz give me all my firsts.

His warm hand ran down my back and cupped my ass. "I'm just getting started. By the time we leave here, there won't be one single inch of your body I haven't touched, licked, and made mine. After tonight no man will ever touch you."

Needing to claim him right back, I leaned forward and licked the flat, dusky disk of his nipple. "This is mine." I moved to his other nipple and then gave it a little nip. "This one too." I moved to sit on top of him. Leaning down, my mouth crashed into his in a kiss that was meant to be me claiming another part of him. Instead, it turned into a slow make-out session with our hands roaming, our tongues tangling together in a sensual dance that had me rubbing against his hard length and coating him with my juices.

Sucking on my bottom lip, Oz's hand slipped around my waist, and he laid me down on the plush bed. He nestled his hips between my legs, his eyes never leaving mine. "All of me is yours. My heart, body, and soul are all yours for the taking. There will never be a time when I want them back."

Oz leaned down, and a condom seemed to appear out of nowhere. "I would love nothing more than to never have a barrier between us, but I understand if that's something you don't want or are willing to risk."

Reaching forward, I took his length in my hand. "I want that too, and I trust you. I've been on the pill since my senior year in high school."

Leaning down, Oz covered my body with his. Strong arms bracketed my head as he ran his thick length along my core. His weight felt like home. Something I'd always needed yet never knew what it was until that moment.

Intertwining our fingers with one hand, he guided his

length to my opening. He pushed himself into me inch by inch until I felt so full; I thought I couldn't take any more of him.

I arched up, trying to accommodate how large he was, and wrapped my arms around his wide shoulders. My breasts flattened against his chest, and the hair on his chest brushed against my nipples.

"This is my first time," he shuddered over me. A look of euphoria washed over his face when he was fully sheathed inside of me. I stretched around his thick length while he gave me time to adjust, but it was his words that took me out of what was going on with my body.

Using my free hand, I ran my hand up the side of his neck and along his chiseled jaw. "Your first time to what?"

"This is the first time for me to make love to someone." He ended his life-altering statement with a deep kiss that filled my body with a love I didn't know I was capable of.

I couldn't wait any longer for him to move. I was desperate as I rocked my hips up, letting Oz know I was ready.

"God, you're beautiful. Every inch of you." He ran his free hand up my stomach and cupped my breast as he started to move.

I couldn't speak with each slow push of his hips. It was as if something was becoming unlocked inside of me. Nothing had ever felt so right or perfect.

My hands roamed over every toned inch of his body I could touch. I never wanted to be apart from Oz again. I would need his touch like I needed air to breathe.

Kissing and nipping up the column of my neck, he extended our joined hands up above my head while his other hand moved expertly down between my legs and made slow, delicious circles on my clit. He kept the same maddening pace that seemed to light up every nerve ending in my body. I was in awe that I was close to detonating in such a short period of time.

Hiking my legs up and wrapping them around his trim waist, I let out a noise I didn't know I was capable of as he went in deeper. At this angle, he was hitting all the right places. With each sensual move, I climbed higher and higher until I plastered my front to his and held on for dear life. I wasn't sure if I was going to be in one piece once I was done, but I didn't care.

"Oz," I moaned his name as I clawed at his back. "I… I…" I couldn't get any coherent words to come out of my mouth between my body lighting up and the noises I was making.

He swiped his thumb over my cheekbone. "I know, baby, and it's okay to let go. I've got you."

And I did just that. I put my body and pleasure into his hands and just felt as Oz picked up the pace, driving himself deeper and deeper inside of me until I couldn't tell where he or I began. We were one from that moment on.

My body started to shake, and I threw my head back as I clasped onto Oz for dear life. Every nerve ending in my body became alive and sang with pleasure. The world went black as I screamed out my release.

When I came back down to Earth, I felt Oz tense up as he buried himself deep inside of me. He dipped his head and let out a low growl next to my ear as I felt his length jerk, and then a warm feeling flooded me.

I held Oz to me as if I was afraid he would float away at any second. I relished in the feel of his heavy breaths as they puffed along my neck and the staccato beat of his heart next to mine.

When his breathing evened out, I thought he fell asleep until he kissed the side of my neck and his head popped up. His blond hair was a sexy mess from my fingers running through it and tugging at the long strands.

He opened his mouth, and if I didn't know before, I knew then Oz was my soulmate. "I love you, Lo. Today, tomorrow, and forever."

Tears filled my eyes as I repeated his words back to him.

EIGHTEEN
OZ

VALENTINE'S DAY

THE FEEL of Lo's naked body pressed against my back as I cooked our dinner had my dick hardening and wanting to be buried deep inside of her for the rest of the night. That was the plan, but first, we needed sustenance.

Her hands roamed along my torso and trailed down dangerously close to cock, only to move up again. "I was scared our first time together was going to be disastrous," Lo said out of nowhere.

I turned in her arms to find her eyes closed as she hung her head. Lifting her chin with my forefinger, I waited until she opened her eyes to speak. "Why would you think that? I always knew we'd be perfect together."

"I knew *you'd* be perfect, but I thought with how inexperienced I am that you might find me boring, or I'd do it wrong." She looked away and blushed, and I couldn't have that.

I hated that she felt she wasn't enough for me. It was another case of my past coming back to bite me in the ass. "And now, how do you feel?"

She pressed her firm breasts against me, and my already hard dick jolted at the contact. I wanted to be back inside her with maddening desperation.

"That I didn't have anything to worry about. I never knew it could be like that. It put all the sex scenes I've read about in romance books to shame."

Wrapping my arms around her, I leaned down and brought our mouths together in a kiss that could only be described as our souls intertwining and connecting on a whole other level.

"I want you to know I've never had sex like that before. All other experiences before you meant nothing, and that was everything." I ran my hand down her back and cupped her ass. "Now that I've been inside of you, be prepared for me to want you every second of every day."

"I like the sound of that," she purred. Her hand trailed

back down, and this time it didn't stop until her fingers were wrapped around my shaft.

"As much as I love you touching me, we should hold off until we get some food in us. Our dinner is almost ready."

Her hand stayed where it was as she looked up at me. "Everything you planned is beyond any fantasy I could have ever dreamed up. This, *everything,* is perfect. Thank you." Her grip on me tightened. "Why don't you finish making our dinner and," her eyes flicked up to meet mine as she licked her lips. I wanted to lean down and take that mouth with mine, but I knew I wouldn't be able to stop. A wicked smirk teased her pink lips. "I'll start on mine."

Before I could question her, Lo sank to her knees before me. Her tongue peeked out and ran along the tip of my cock. "You taste good," she moaned before sucking my head into her hot, wet mouth.

I tried to make sure our dinner didn't burn, but all thoughts of food were forgotten as Lo took more of my length between her pouty lips. She bobbed up and down and used her hand on what she couldn't take, nearly bringing me to my knees. With each swipe of her tongue around my head, I almost unleashed inside her mouth.

When one of her hands moved between her legs, and she moaned around my length, I knew I couldn't hold back any longer.

"I'm close," I moaned. "If you don't want…"

Lo opened wider and swallowed until my cock hit the back of her throat, and I was done for. I let go and watched as she tried to drink all of me down. A little cum slipped out of the corner of her mouth, and I nearly came again. Lo on her knees, naked before me as she touched herself while drinking down my cum would be ingrained into my brain for the rest of my life as one of the hottest things I ever saw.

Holding out my hand, I helped her up and pulled her to me. My mouth slanted over hers, and I tasted the saltiness of my release mixed with her unique taste on her tongue. I sucked her tongue into my mouth and devoured her until we were both breathless and needed to come up for air.

"Oz," Lo giggled and pointed to the stove.

The sauce that I'd been so carefully stirring before was starting to bubble over the pan.

"Does that mean dinner's ready?" She arched a brow at me.

"It does, and if it's burned, it was all worth it to see you before me taking my cock between those lips of yours." I ran my thumb along her bottom lip. Lo's tongue licked the tip and then sucked my thumb into her mouth. "As enticing as you are with that mouth of yours, let me feed you."

She was making it difficult to not think with only my dick. Luckily, the need to take care of her won out. Helping her to her feet, I guided Lo over to the counter before draping a blanket I found on the back of the couch around her shoulders.

"Where did you learn how to cook? I don't think I've ever seen you in front of a stove," she sat down on a stool and watched me as I tried to save the sauce.

"I picked it up from my mom, mostly. You saw how we eat for football, and now Ford cooks for us as his way of paying rent. There hasn't been a reason for me to do much cooking." I shrugged. "I'm not saying I'm good, but I can make a decent meal."

She hummed, and I wasn't sure if it was from watching me make our dinner naked or that I might be able to cook.

"If you don't like it, it won't hurt my feelings. There's plenty of other food here, but for tonight, I wanted to make you something with my own two hands." I probably would be hurt if she didn't like my food, but I'd play it off. Nothing was going to ruin this weekend.

Putting the steaks on our plates, I spooned the sauce over them and then pulled the rolls out of the oven. I made both of our plates with loaded mashed potatoes and asparagus.

Lo looked down at her plate and then up at me. "I can't believe you made all of this. It smells and looks so good. Does this mean you'll be the cook in this relationship?"

Pride swelled inside of me. I'd cook her every meal of the day for as long as she wanted if she looked at me with the same amount of wonder in her eyes as she was in that moment.

"If that's what you want. Although you'll soon find out my cooking is pretty limited," I admitted. "I can make a mean bowl of cereal and heat up a meal with the best of them."

Lo shook her head. "I don't believe you. Maybe we can learn together. It's either that or we're going to starve."

"I think we'll make do. It might not be gourmet, but we won't starve." I watched as she spooned up some of the mashed potatoes to see if they were any good.

She gave me a side-eye as she chewed. "I feel like you're punking me with the way you're looking at me. Is there something wrong with the food?"

"I wouldn't do that to you. Tonight," I amended. "Maybe on a different day, but not on Valentine's Day."

"With each date, I think you'll never be able to top the date we're on, and yet you do. Every single time." She reached out and laced our fingers together. "You're a good boyfriend."

Little did she know, I was constantly trying to plan our next date and how to make them special. I knew I didn't deserve Lo, and I knew once I heard from Tori, which could be at any moment, there was the potential of her turning our world upside down.

NINETEEN

LO

END OF FEBRUARY

WALKING BACK to the house from Charlie's walk, I saw Fin running toward me down the street. While we got along, for the most part, he was not one to come for a walk with us, which put me on high alert. Charlie tugged on his leash, excited to see Fin, and thought he wanted to play.

"What's wrong?" I asked when we were within a few feet of each other.

Fin looked relieved the moment I spoke. "Dean's on his way. Oz is freaking out, and he's worried Dean might show up while you are out here and do something to you."

"Why didn't he come find me?"

"Because he's out of his mind," he held his arms out to his sides and let them fall. "If Dean shows up while you two are out here, who knows what could happen. In fact, it might be best if you left. That way, you can't be used against Oz."

"Not happening," I shook my head as I continued making my way back to the house. "There's no way in hell I'm letting him deal with this all by himself."

"What am I, chopped liver? I'll be there along with West and Ford. We won't let anything happen to him. It hasn't escaped our notice how much better Oz has been since he confessed to everything. Let's keep it that way. You can come back home once everything is over."

It didn't matter what anyone said; I was not leaving. I had to stand by my man. And Oz was better, but he was also still on edge, waiting for Tori to show up and Dean to call. His life was in limbo until both of them were taken care of.

I whirled around to face Fin. "Did Oz ask you to get me to leave, so he didn't have to?"

Fin didn't stop walking. In fact, he sped up as we neared the house. "Do you even know me? I'm doing this for him because I don't want him to do something he'll regret because he's trying to protect you."

I didn't want that either, but I couldn't leave.

I'd barely stepped onto the front porch when the door swung open, and Oz pulled me into the house. His hands ran over my body and his eyes traced over where his hands were in case he missed something.

"Are you okay?" He asked, exhaling a heavy breath.

"I'm fine. I was just out walking Charlie." I grabbed his hands and held them between mine. "The better question is, are you okay?"

"I will be once all this shit is over. I'm tired of Dean and Tori's bullshit hanging over everything I do."

I knew Oz was worried about what might happen if the baby Tori was carrying was his. I hadn't let myself think about it. Every time the thought popped up in my mind, I became nauseous. I couldn't sit around and do all the what-ifs because it would drive me crazy. I had to wait until we knew for sure, but I was confident we could weather whatever storm we faced.

It would more than sting—if Oz had a child that wasn't mine, but I wasn't willing to give him up. Not now.

A car door slammed outside, and the next thing I knew, I was in Oz's arms as he carried me into our bedroom and sat me down by the bed. "What are you doing?"

"I don't want him to set eyes on you. If Dean knows my weakness, he could target you." He sat me down by the bed and then wrapped me in his arms. "No, he will, and I can't have that. There's no way in the world I could ever put you in any danger."

"Fine, I'll stay in here if it will make you feel better," I mumbled into his chest.

"Thank you. I'll get Charlie back here with you." He pushed back to look down at me. "You can write that paper you've been putting off."

He was delusional if he thought for one minute I was going to be able to concentrate on my homework while he was out there dealing with Dean.

"Hey," Fin called from the doorway. "It wasn't him, so you can come out now."

Grabbing Oz's hand, I pulled him out to the living room. "We've got to have a better strategy than to hide me. None of you mentioned it when we talked about it before. Was this always the plan?" I turned, narrowing my eyes at each of the guys, and kept them on Oz once I got to him.

"Now that we know he's coming, things changed. Where we are today compared where we were then is miles apart." Oz moved to me and buried his face in the crook of my neck. "I can't lose you."

"You won't." I'd do whatever he needed me to, but until then, I was going to be by his side.

We sat waiting on the couch for the next three hours, waiting for Dean to show up and jumping at every sound.

Ford stood up and headed into the kitchen. "Well, I'm going to making dinner. You know, maybe he was just pulling your chain, or he's waiting for you to let your guard down, and then he'll show up."

"Or maybe he heard you were going to go to the cops and wanted to see if it was true. He could be watching us or having someone else watching," West said, making cold fear run through my blood.

"How would he know that?" Oz jumped up and started pacing. "The only people who know are us."

"Well, where the hell is he? It's been hours and no Dean," West shot back.

A sharp knock sounded on the front door, causing us all to jump. Oz's blue eyes widened as he looked at me. I knew what I needed to do. I grabbed Charlie's collar and led him to the bedroom, where I closed the door almost all the way but left it open enough that I could hear what was happening out in the living room.

"Is one of you Oz Francisco?" I heard an unfamiliar voice ask.

"That's me," Oz answered. "Can I help you, officer?"

"I certainly hope so. We found a vehicle that was involved in a deadly collision. The VIN was scraped clean, and the plates aren't registered to the car, making it difficult to identify the victim in the accident."

"How can we help?" West asked.

I moved with my ear to the open door, trying to hear better.

"I believe you can." The officer started loudly, but then his voice dropped. I opened the door further now that I knew it wasn't Dean who had shown up. "We found this address with the name of Oz Francisco on a piece of paper. We'd like to notify the next of kin to identify the body, and that's where you come in. Did you have someone coming to visit?"

Next of kin? Body?

Someone was dead.

"Well, we thought we did, but he was no friend of ours. He called earlier and said he was coming but never showed up," West supplied.

"What was the make and model of the car you found?" Fin jumped in, sounding more authoritative than the police officer.

"Boy, I'm the one asking questions here," the officer huffed. I guess he didn't like Fin taking over.

"Well, I'm not sure if we'll be able to help you then if you can't even tell us the car. We have many friends, and it could have been any number of them coming to visit. Should we make a list of all of our friends and their car models?"

Not wanting Fin to get arrested, I stepped out into the hall and walked silently to the front door, where all four guys were standing at attention.

"And who is this?" The officer's eyes landed on me, and I froze in place. "Do you by any chance know who might have been coming here with this address and the name Oz Francisco scribbled on a piece of paper?"

"Not particularly. It could have been Oz's sister," I threw out and then realized how stupid that sounded. Why would Dani write Oz's name on a piece of paper, and even if she did, she wouldn't put their last name on it. "Really, officer, I don't know. Did you find a car?" I asked, like I hadn't been listening to the entire conversation.

The squat, stalky man exhaled loudly. "I can see I'm going to get nowhere with any of you. Let me go out to my cruiser and find out the make and model of the vehicle involved in the crash, and maybe that will refresh your memory."

We all watched in silence as the policeman walked to the end of the driveway and sat down in the driver's seat.

Fin's dark eyes landed on Oz. "Do you think it was Dean? Could we be that lucky that he died on the way here?"

"No one said he was dead," Oz mumbled as he continued to watch the officer.

Fin moved, so he was blocking Oz's view. His eyes narrowed. "He used the words body and identifying the victim. If that doesn't mean someone's dead, then I don't know what it means."

"Does Dean have more than one car?" Ford asked, moving from foot to foot.

Oz held out his hand, and I went to him, taking his hand

and weaving our fingers together. "I've only seen him in the one. It's a black Honda Civic with blacked-out windows."

"Then let's hope that's what he comes back with, and you'll have one less problem to deal with. Maybe Tori was with him, and she's gone too."

We all turned to Fin with wide eyes, but it was West who spoke. "I know you want to protect your friend, but don't wish death on anyone. While Dean is most definitely a bad person, neither he nor Tori deserve to die."

"Fine, whatever you say," Fin rolled his eyes and then pinned Oz with his gaze. "You can't say it wouldn't make your life easier."

"It would," Oz nodded. "But damn, dude, be a decent human being."

Ford and West straightened, and the rest of us followed. The police officer scowled at us as he walked up the porch steps.

"Do any of you know anyone who drives a two thousand and ten black Honda Civic?"

If we were going to try to lie, we failed by all turning to look at Oz.

"I do," Oz stepped forward, letting go of my hand. I wanted to step forward and take his hand back, but this wasn't about me, even if I wanted to be here for him. "His name is Dean Forrester. He lives in my hometown of Santa Lucia."

"See, that wasn't so hard, now was it?" He looked us up and down and started to turn before he spoke. "I hope whatever it is your friend was coming to see you about doesn't come back to bite you in the ass."

What the hell was with his guy? He was the worst policeman I'd ever encountered. This lawman was the type that made people not trust the police.

"Was there anyone else in the car by any chance?" Fin stepped forward and asked.

The policeman cocked his head and then shook it. "Were you expecting someone else to be in the car?"

"No, sir," Oz answered, pushing Fin back inside the house before he closed the door and locked it. We all stood there looking out the window, waiting for the officer to drive away. Once he was gone, Oz slumped against the door and slid down until his ass hit the floor.

I moved to sit beside Oz, resting my head on his shoulder. Wanting him to be able to process what we learned, I kept quiet. Fin reached out and patted Oz on the shoulder before he and West left the room.

Ford looked between us and gave me a half-smile. "I'll be in my room if you need me."

"Thanks," I answered back before I turned and wrapped myself around Oz. Charlie ambled down the hallway and stepped between us to lick Oz's cheek.

Pulling Charlie into his chest, Oz hugged him and then

rested his head on top of mine. He let out a deep exhale. "What do you say we go to bed? I'm wiped."

I nodded and started to get up, only for Oz to pull me down onto his lap. His mouth met mine in a desperate kiss that I eagerly gave into.

Pulling back, I sucked on his bottom lip and then rested my forehead against his. "Take me to bed."

Without any effort, Oz stood with me in his arms. Wrapping my legs around his waist, I kissed along his jaw as he walked us to our bedroom. Closing and locking the door seemed to be as far as Oz was willing to take us into the room. He pressed me up against the door as his hands went to the hem of my shirt and pulled it over my head.

"Have I ever told you how much I love that you don't wear a bra around the house?" He growled before taking one nipple between his teeth and tugging.

My back arched into the pleasure and pain as one hand snaked into his hair and held him in place.

"How much do you like these pants?" His hands went to the sides of my yoga pants and waited for my answer.

Right then, I hated any offending garment that kept Oz away from me. "Do what you have to do," I mumbled against the skin beneath his ear.

Moving his hands between my legs, Oz ripped the crotch out of my leggings and then swiped his fingers through my already damp folds.

"Fucking hell, you were made for me," he said between well-placed kisses and nips along my collarbone. Grinding against my stomach and then running his length along my exposed pussy, Oz groaned. "I need to be inside you."

"I need you too." My hands moved to his sweatpants, pulled his hard length out, and placed him at my entrance.

With one hard thrust, Oz was buried deep inside of me. He didn't give me time to adjust. Instead, he pulled almost all the way out and then slammed back inside me. He hit places inside of me I didn't know existed with each deep penetrating move of his hips.

I dug my heels into his ass as I pulled his shirt over his head and then used his hair to pull him down to my aching breasts. Not needing any more direction, Oz took one peeked nipple into his mouth. With each suck and swirl of his tongue, I felt the pull deep in my core.

My walls started to flutter, seeming to spur Oz on more. One hand skated down between the apex of my thighs, and when his thumb grazed my clit, I nearly shot into the stratosphere.

"Oh God, more," I moaned, bucking into his touch.

I didn't think it was possible, but Oz picked up his pace, pistoning his hips until all I could hear was the harsh sound of our labored breathing and the slap of our skin.

"I need you to come for me," he grunted out, jerking his hips. I felt him grow inside me, and then the hot splash of his cum filling me from deep inside set me off. My entire body clutched around him as I rode his length until I was spent and breathless in Oz's arms.

Lifting his head, Oz smiled lazily at me. He moved us over to the bed, where he laid me down and then stripped off my now ruined leggings. I watched his ass as he walked out of the room and came back inside with a warm, wet washcloth. Sitting down on the side of the bed, he wiped between my legs and then threw the washcloth in the hamper by the closet.

Instead of moving to the other side of the bed, Oz laid down beside me and curled into me, pulling me against him until every inch of me was touching every spectacular inch of him. I rested my head against his chest and listened to his breathing slowly start to even out.

"I love you," he said quietly before he fell asleep.

"I love you," I kissed the space between his pecs and then nuzzled into his chest to fall asleep.

THE MOMENT I woke up and my eyes popped open, I found Oz leaning up against the headboard with his laptop on his stomach, looking at the local news website. His brows were pulled together, and his usual blue eyes were dark like a storm was brewing in them.

Rolling toward him, I ran my hand up his arm. "Is everything okay?"

His troubled eyes met mine and then went back to the computer. "It says they found drugs in the car and suspect Dean was high at the time of his accident. I'm not sure how to feel about this. I'm happy I don't have to worry about Dean anymore. Does that make me a bad person?"

Pulling him down to me, I wrapped my arms around his broad shoulders and held on tight as Oz buried his face into my neck. He held onto me just as strongly as I held him.

"It doesn't make you a bad person. He was the bad guy, terrorizing your life. It's only natural to feel relieved you don't have to worry about what he's going to do next. If you were a bad person, you wouldn't be asking if what you're thinking makes you a bad person. You wouldn't care."

He nodded as his hot breath bathed the side of my neck. "He said he was coming for money even when I said I didn't have any. That I'd pay one way or another, and all I could think about is what if he hurt you." Oz let out a shaky breath.

"But we're both fine," I said as I ran my fingers through the soft strands of his hair.

He raised up, resting on his elbows as not to smush me. "Tomorrow, I'm calling Tori and demanding a paternity test. I can't keep moving through life with all the what-ifs. I have to know."

"I know you do, and if it is your baby, it won't be ideal, but we'll deal with it."

"I don't want it to be." The tremble in his voice had tears welling up in my eyes. "I've only wanted to have a baby with you, and now I may have I've ruined that for us. If I am the father, I won't be some deadbeat." He moved down and laid his head on my stomach. "I know it will put a strain on us. It will be a constant reminder that I fucked up, and you weren't the mother of my child."

He was right, it would be difficult, but if we were meant to be together, then we'd make this just like everything else.

TWENTY
OZ

MARCH

I TRIED TO SWALLOW, but my throat was too dry. My hand shook as I pressed the button to take me up to the fifth floor of the hospital. Lo stood resiliently beside me with her head held high and her eyes focused on the door. I knew this couldn't be easy for her, but she never wavered when I asked her if she wanted to stay back in Willow Bay.

I'd called Tori the day after the policeman showed up asking about Dean, and she didn't answer or bother to call me back for two days. She went into labor late last night and demanded that I get here immediately with her money. Just thinking about it made me scoff. Seriously, how delusional was she that she thought I'd blindly give her money?

Lo's warm hand wrapped around mine as she whispered. "Are you okay?"

"Not really," I answered as the elevator came to a stop.

"Why don't we go by and see the babies before heading to her room?" she suggested. I didn't see the point, but I didn't want to face Tori either, so I let Lo guide me to the nursery. We stopped in front of a large window that showcased around twelve babies with little pink and blue hats on their heads. "What's Tori's last name?"

The thing was, I had no idea what her last name was. I wasn't in the mood to get to know her when I was drunk and supposedly hooking up with her.

Turning away from all the babies, I pulled our hands up to kiss the back of her hand. "Will you think badly of me if I don't know?"

"No, but it would be helpful to know. If you want, I can go scope out Tori's room to see what her last name is. That way, we can... you know." She nodded her head toward the window.

I did know. To see what my potential child looked like. Before I could answer her, Lo was taking off in the direction of the rooms. Turning back to the window, I looked in, trying to see if any of them looked like me, but they all looked like little old men with their wrinkly red faces.

"Okay," Lo panted as she came up beside me. "I got her last name. It's Smith," she wrinkled her nose. "Do you think she gave a fake last name?"

"Not really. Why?"

"Because who has the last name of Smith anymore? It's so... generic." Putting both hands on the window, Lo scanned the room. "The baby should have the same name unless she gave them yours."

My stomach dropped to the floor at the thought. The only people I wanted to have my last name were Lo and *our* future children.

"I don't see any Francisco's," she murmured against the glass. "Is that a Smith?"

Shaking my head out of my depressing thoughts, I looked to where she was pointing. I squinted my eyes, trying to see the name, but it was the last row, making it difficult.

"Yes, can you help us?" I heard Lo say. She had a phone receiver up to her ear, pointing in the direction of the one we thought was Smith. "Can we see Tori Smith's baby?" She paused for a moment and nodded. "Yeah, we can wait."

Lo hung up the phone and turned to me. "She's going to bring the baby up to the window so that we can see it better."

"I'm sorry for putting you through this. I understand if it's too much," I word-vomited. "You don't deserve to have this be your life."

Stepping to me, Lo rested her head against my chest. My

arms went around her petite frame and hugged her to me. "Neither do you," she answered back with a hug of her own.

There was a tap on the glass, making us turn to see a nurse stepping out of the way of a baby that was most definitely not mine. Whoever the father was, he had a darker complexion than mine.

"That's not your baby," Lo croaked out.

Moving to stand behind her, I wrapped my arms around her shoulders and pulled her back to my front. "Are you sure you got the right last name?"

"I'm positive. I double-checked, and the nurse confirmed a Tori Smith. Did she think even for a second that the baby would come out so obviously not looking anything like either of you?"

I think she was hoping I'd give her more money to never be a part of the baby's life. "I think it's time for me to go visit Tori and see what she has to say."

"Why?" Lo pulled on my hand to stop me.

"Because she's put me through hell for months, telling me that we had sex and that I got her pregnant when I couldn't even remember it. It's obvious now why I don't remember any of it. I was set up, and it was probably all Dean's idea. Those two assholes probably conspired against me to take all my money." With each word I said, the more I believed it.

I took off down the hall, ready to confront Tori. The worst part was she could have cost me Lo, and if that had happened, I'm not sure what I would have done.

Lo came running up beside me. "What are you going to do?"

"I'm going to confront her. Well, first, I'll pretend I didn't just see a child that couldn't possibly be mine, and then I'll drop the bomb. Does she think I'm stupid?" I growled out as I stalked toward Tori's room.

A nurse was coming out of the room and slunk away when she saw me coming. I didn't blame her. I was on the warpath, and I was sure I looked it as well.

"Oz," Tori sighed out my name in a breathy whisper that sent my blood boiling. "I didn't know when you'd show up, but I was hoping it was before I went home with our son."

"Oh, we have a son, do we? Have you seen him yet? Does he have my nose or my hair?"

"I… um… I saw him after I gave birth, but he was all messy, and I was exhausted after pushing for hours. I really wanted you to be here for the birth of our son, though. You're always going to wish you'd been there."

Oh, I was sure I'd regret not being there to see the look on her face when her baby came out, and knowing that the second I saw him, I would figure out she'd been playing me the entire time.

She looked out the window and then to me as she chewed the inside of her cheek. "They said I'm going to have to pay before I leave. I'm going to need help, and since this is half your fault, I think you should pay half."

It took everything within me to keep from laughing or from wrapping my hands around her neck and strangling her to death. Lo choked on a laugh behind me, causing Tori to finally realize someone else was in the room.

"Who is that?" She tried to peer around me from the bed, but neither Lo nor I moved. "Is that Dani?"

"No, that's my girlfriend. She came along for emotional support and to make sure that we do a DNA test today because there's no way in hell I'm paying you another dime until I know with one hundred percent certainty that the child is mine."

"What?" Tori screeched. "You can't do that. It will take days, if not a week, to find out the results from a paternity test."

"Well, I guess you should have called me back instead of avoiding me until you went into labor." I gave her a fake frown and then turned away. "Anyway, I already gave you money for an abortion you didn't have, so you do have money from me to use."

"Don't be that way, Oz. Please," she begged. "I used that money for my doctor's visits and to eat healthy once I knew I couldn't give up our baby."

I was sure she used the money on anything but doctor care while she was pregnant.

"I think I'll head down to the nursery now and ask them to do a DNA test while I'm here. That way, I won't have to see you again until after I get the results back." I started to walk out of the room, barely able to keep the smile off my face, when Tori shouted.

"Wait, Oz. You don't have to do this. I just need help paying the hospital bill, and after that, we can do the DNA test. Do you really want to have your son poked by a needle when he's only a day old?"

"Why does his age matter? It will still happen no matter what, and I think it would be more traumatizing the older he gets. Anyway, I want to see my son. I bet he looks just like me. Isn't that what they say 'bout newborns? They look just like their dad so he will accept them?"

"But you don't need to. You're such a good guy, and I know you already love him. I thought we could name him Oz Junior."

Moving back toward the bed, I took her in. Her eyes were wide with fear, and her face was paler than normal. "You do know that we know nothing about each other, right? I mean, I didn't even know what your last name was until today, and you obviously don't know what my first name is because if you did, you'd never want to name your child after me." Oswald was such an old man's name and I hated it with a passion.

"Of course, I want to name him after his father," she scrambled to sit up straighter in her bed.

"Then you better figure out who the real fucking father is because it sure as shit isn't me. I already went down to the nursery and asked to see your baby. You know what was strange when I saw him?" I didn't give her a chance to answer. "I'm sure you do. *Your* son has dark hair and skin. He doesn't look like either one of us, so I'm guessing he looks like his real daddy and not the man you're trying to make an imposter."

"You're wrong! Babies don't always look like their parents at first when they're born, but if you give it time, he'll look just like you."

"What, after you switch him with another baby? No thanks. I don't want to be an accomplice to your evil ways any longer." My nostrils flared as I stepped even closer to the bed. With each step, Tori tried to sink further into the bed. "I don't know why you picked me to target and try to ruin, but it's not going to happen. You can't play me anymore. In fact, I'm almost a hundred percent positive we never had sex that night."

"You're probably still a virgin," she laughed maniacally. "You've been waiting around since the moment *she* moved here to dip your wick in her. You're absolutely pathetic," she snarled. "And probably a lousy lay. If I were you, I'd run far, far away from him and his sad little dick."

Lo stepped around me and over to the side of the bed. For a second, I thought she was going to be sweet to Tori. That was until she opened her mouth.

"I'll have you know that I love that man," she pointed to me. "And his dick is phenomenal, and every night he gives me the best orgasms of my life. So really, it's you who missed out. Now, if you don't mind, I'm going to take my man and get out of here, so he can supply me with more orgasms than you can hope to achieve in your lifetime."

Turning on her heel, Lo hooked her arm with mine and dragged me out of Tori's hospital room. I broke out into laughter the second we were out in the hallway. I knew Tori could hear me, but I couldn't stop. "I can't believe you said that."

"I can't either, but it's true," Lo laughed with me as she hit the button for the elevator. "Now we can practice for when we have a baby of our own in the distant future."

I waited until the doors to the elevator opened up and boxed Lo in against the wall, pressing my growing erection into her stomach. Leaning down, I ran my tongue up the side of her neck and bit down on the fleshy part of her earlobe. "You should be prepared to have twins. It runs in my family."

Running her hands up my arms to clasp around my neck,

Lo looked up at me with so much love and devotion in her eyes it was staggering. I knew then I'd do anything for her, and one day, I would marry her. Her delicate fingers drifted through the long strands of my hair as she spoke. "I'm prepared for anything with you by my side."

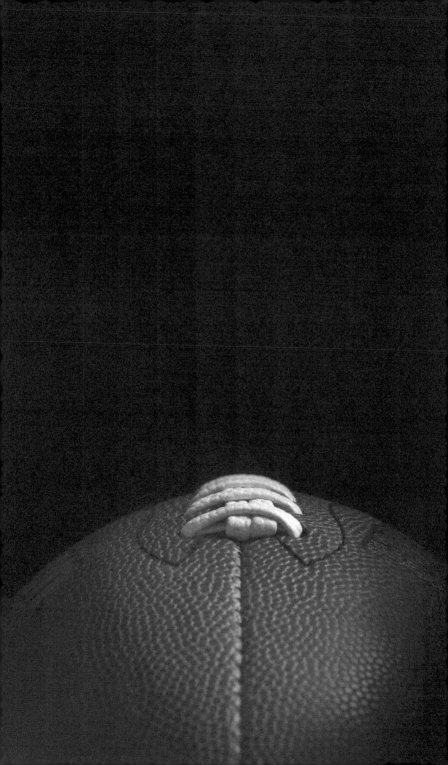

EPILOGUE

LO
JULY

"IS THAT WHAT YOU'RE WEARING?" Fin eyed me up and down as I slipped on a pair of black peep-toe heels.

What was with him always asking this every time I went on a date with Oz?

"Uh, yeah. Do I look bad?" I asked, looking down at the blue dress that matched the color of my eyes. It was form-fitting, showing off every curve. Something I thought Oz would appreciate.

Fin's face scrunched up. "Not bad, but do you have

anything *nicer*?"

"What's the big deal about tonight? It's just our typical date night, and you all are making it seem like I'm going to be on TV, and I'm not ready for it. If you fill me in, maybe I can wear the appropriate outfit."

"I'm not sure what the right outfit for tonight would be. This really isn't my specialty," Fin shook his head.

I wanted to ask him what his specialty was besides being an asshole, but I was always told you catch more flies with honey than vinegar. I bit back what I wanted to say.

I huffed, blowing a piece of hair out of my face, and placed my hands on my hips. "Well, if no one will tell me what the hell is going on, this is what I'm going to wear, and if it's not good enough, then it's your fault, not mine."

Fin leaned back against the wall and crossed his arms over his chest. "What do you think he's been working his ass off for all summer long? It's not so you two can get your own place," Fin laughed darkly.

Oz had been working with Fin all summer trying to make back some of the money he'd been blackmailed into giving Dean, but he wouldn't tell me why. I knew he'd be getting the next installment of his trust fund money at the end of summer, so it didn't make sense to me. All Oz would tell me was he was the man, and he wasn't going to let me pay for everything. He'd been waiting forever to date me, and he wanted to be able to pay for those dates and give me gifts whenever he felt like it. It was our first and only fight so far, with the exception of me finding out Tori was pregnant. After Oz explained, I gave in after seeing how exhausted he was one night after he and Fin got home from a long day at work. While I didn't understand the complex nature of a man's ego–let alone Oz's–I resigned myself to seeing a lot less of him for the duration of the summer and letting Oz be the one to pay for our dates.

Now I was wondering why Oz was so determined to work his fingers to the bone. I hadn't asked for anything. Only for him to give me one night a week where we could do something with just the two of us. It didn't even have to require money. We headed to the bay most of the time, where we sat and watched the tide come in and made love under the stars. It was free and perfect, with no ears listening in.

So why did he need money?

"Is he buying a new car?" Fin rolled his eyes and walked away. Maybe Oz was saving up money to renovate the basement so that we could have a space all to ourselves. Whatever it was, it shouldn't matter what I wore tonight.

"I hate you. You know that?" I yelled at his retreating form. "Why bring it up if you're not going to tell me?"

Fin didn't even bother to turn around to look at me as he spoke. "Because I thought you were smart enough to figure it out on your own. Tonight is a special occasion whether you know it or not, and that's all I'm going to say." He walked into his bedroom and closed the door, letting me know he truly was done speaking to me.

It was then Oz walked in the front door with a happy Charlie by his side. He was hanging the leash when I asked. "Do I look okay?"

Oz stopped what he was doing, and even from down the hall, I could tell he liked what he saw. His eyes went half-mast as a sexy smile took over his handsome face. "You're absolutely gorgeous. I can't wait to peel that dress off you later."

"Is it appropriate for where we're going?" Fin had me so unnerved I was second-guessing everything.

"Yeah, why wouldn't it be?" He looked down at his dark-washed jeans and shirt. "Do I look okay? I know I'm a little bit sweaty from our walk, but I'll clean up a little."

"You look very dashing. Even sweaty. Especially sweaty in some cases." I grinned, thinking of Oz sweating as he hovered over me and thrust inside.

He stalked toward me and didn't stop until he was flush to me. "Oh, we'll be getting sweaty like that by the end of the night. Let me go get cleaned up real quick, and then we can leave." Leaning down, Oz kissed me like he'd never get to kiss me again. With each swipe of his tongue, I could feel his want and desperation between us.

"If you two keep that up, there won't be a date," Fin

grumbled as he walked into the kitchen.

Oz pulled away and laughed. "You're an asshole. You know that?"

"Tell me something I don't know," Fin shot back.

"What's up his ass, or maybe I should say what's not up his ass?" Oz laughed.

"Oz," I slapped his arm as I looked toward the kitchen, hoping Fin hadn't heard what Oz had just said. "Don't say things like that."

"Why? He's my best friend, and he has a boyfriend. If you think nothing has been up his ass, you're wrong."

Fin leaned across the kitchen counter. His dark eyes narrowed at us. "Is your sex life so boring that you have to discuss mine?"

"I'm sorry, Fin." I walked over and placed my hand on his arm, but I removed it when he looked down at my hand with a blank face. "He shouldn't have said anything. What you and West do is your own business. I know I wouldn't like it if you were discussing what goes on between us."

"Then maybe you two should keep it down while in the shower. You seem to forget that the walls here are thin." He pushed off the counter and looked down at me. "Before you go, West and I were wondering if either of you has heard from Ford since he left to go home for the summer."

"Not me, but I don't even have his phone number." I turned to look at Oz.

"I texted him a couple of times and got back a vague response." Oz slipped his arm around my waist. "Do you think something's up with him?"

Fin shrugged like he didn't care. "West hasn't gotten much of a response from him and thought he'd be back by now since practice starts next week."

"I'm sure he'll be back before practice starts. If you're worried, you could ask Coach Kyle if he's heard anything."

"I'm not worried," Fin scoffed. "And why the hell would Coach know? He doesn't keep tabs on us during the summer."

"Well, some of us don't have dinner with Coach at least once a month," Oz grumbled. "I'll text him tomorrow and let you know if I hear back from him. Now, I'm going to take my beautiful girlfriend on our date, so don't wait up."

"Trust me, I won't wait up," Fin clapped Oz on the shoulder. "We're going to have our own date night, right here, but you two have fun." Fin winked before he moved back into the kitchen. "Ford really needs to come home because I'm tired of making my own crappy dinner."

Only Fin would deflect missing Ford with talk of cooking his own meals.

"I'll be right back," Oz kissed my forehead and then headed to the bathroom.

"Thank you for trying to help me tonight, even though you left me in the dark. Your friendship means a lot to Oz and to me," I nodded, wanting Fin to know I considered him a friend. "You didn't have to take me in, but you did, and I'm thankful."

"I didn't do anything," he grumbled.

"You may not realize it, but you did, and you still do, so thank you." Stepping forward, I hugged him, but only briefly. Fin stood there the entire time, ramrod straight, clearly uncomfortable. "Thank you," I said again before I released him from my hold.

Fin looked at me like I'd grown two heads. Wanting to give him his space, I decided to wait by the door. A couple of minutes later, we were sitting in Oz's car.

"What was that about with you and Fin?" Oz asked the moment he pulled out of the driveway.

"Nothing. I was just thanking him for taking me in and for being a good friend to you. You know he's worried about Ford, right?"

"You don't have to tell me," Oz laughed. "Fin is one stubborn son-of-a-bitch, and he'll never admit it. Maybe if it was West, and even then, I don't know."

"So, where are we going?" I asked, hoping Oz would finally try not to surprise me.

"To Bay Grill. I thought it would be nice for us to go back to the place where we had our first date." He looked over at me and then back to the road while biting his bottom lip.

"That was a romantic night," I leaned over and kissed his cheek. "Why do I feel like there's something special about tonight?"

Oz looked at me from the corner of his eye. "Every night with you is special, but I am hoping for tonight to be a little something extra."

Why tonight?

I wracked my brain trying to figure out what was so special about today, but nothing came to mind. Our first date was in January, and I didn't come to stay in Willow Bay until August. In all the years I'd known Oz, nothing of any significance had happened in July.

"And does everyone know about what's happening tonight except me?" I questioned curiously.

"Why are you asking me all these questions?" He chuckled. "Did someone say something?"

"Fin alluded that my dress wasn't nice enough for whatever's happening, but that's all. He made it seem like I should have already figured it out."

Oz frowned as he stared out the windshield. "Well, Fin doesn't know what the hell he's talking about. That dress is one thousand percent perfect for tonight. Don't mind anything he said. He's being extra moody lately."

"Why? Because he's worried about Ford?"

Oz scoffed. "Doubtful. Probably because he's going to have to start working less, which means less money, along with football and school. He's an asshole when he's stressed."

Well, he must be stressed all the damn time then.

"Let's forget about everything but us tonight," Oz reached over and laced our fingers together. "Deal? I want to enjoy spending the night with my beautiful girlfriend before football and school start back up."

"I'm always happy to spend time with you, no matter where we are. I have to confess; I am a little nervous about going to classes in person. I don't know anyone here but Fin, West, and Ford. And of course, you," I grasped onto his hand tighter.

"You'll meet people once class starts, and you've always got us. If you need anything, let me or the guys know."

I nodded that I would as we pulled up in front of the restaurant. The sun was close to setting, and it amazed me that once again, Oz had managed to pick the perfect time.

He jumped out of the car like his ass was on fire as he came around to my side and opened my door for me.

"Thank you," I smiled up at him, taking his offered hand.

Guiding me by the small of my back, Oz ran his other hand down my arm and around the curve of my hip. He leaned down and kissed the skin just below my ear. "It's my pleasure."

Shivers danced down my spine. My body so easily reacted to his touch and words.

"Reservation for two, Francisco," Oz said to the woman who was behind the hostess station, pulling me against his front with his hands on my hips.

"Oh, yes," the brunette exclaimed as she rushed around the station. "We have everything ready for you just as you requested."

I thought maybe he'd reserved the same table for us, but I couldn't have been more wrong as we followed the hostess to the back of the restaurant and then out the back. Couples were sitting outside on the deck, but we passed by all of them and down a set of stairs. I started to worry about walking on the sand until I saw a walkway that led down to the water. There was a small pier that I hadn't realized was here before now, with one lone table sitting out on it.

"Is that for us?" I pointed to the table in wonder.

"All for us for and for as long as we want," he smiled down at me, but I got a sense of nervousness coming from him.

"This is perfect, and it's all too much," I turned to him, lifting one hand to cup his smooth cheek. "I don't want you spending everything you made this summer on one night with me when we have the rest of our lives together."

"Don't you worry about my money problems. Tonight isn't costing much more than it did on our first date, but if you don't start walking, our hostess is going to think something's wrong."

"We can't have that, can we," I grabbed his hand as I took off for our own private pier.

"Is everything set up to your liking?" The hostess asked with a timid smile, making me wonder if it was her who set it all up.

Oz looked around our space and then nodded. "It's perfect. Thank you." He pulled out my chair and waited for me to sit before he pushed it in.

"Your server will be with you shortly," she said before heading back up to the restaurant.

Oz sat down beside me, remembering how I asked to sit side by side with him the first time we ate here. Running my hand up his arm until I curled it around his bicep, I rested my head against his shoulder. "You spoil me. Thank you for this. I know the night has only just begun, but I think it's going to be my favorite date of all time."

"Good, that's what I was going for."

Looking back to the restaurant and seeing how far away it was. You could barely make out the people on the deck, which made me bold. I ran my hand up the inside of Oz's thigh. "Do you think we could have sex out here?"

Oz pulled back, only to lean down and take my mouth in a kiss that had my panties instantly wet. Our tongues lashed feverishly at the others as we both moaned. I gripped him by the shoulders, needing more, but stopped when he pulled away, panting.

"As much as it kills me to say this," he picked up my hand and placed it on the bulge in his pants. "I think we should wait until it's at least dark."

He was probably right, even if I didn't want to admit it.

"Fine," I pouted. "But once it's dark, I'm going to ride you like my own personal mechanical bull." I gave his cock a squeeze and then moved back over to my side.

"I look forward to it, but for now, we should decide on dinner, so the waiter doesn't have to come back multiple times. I want to be interrupted the least amount of times possible tonight," he winked.

"I like the way you think." Leaning over, I kissed him on his jaw. "This is already the most special date of my life. Seriously, I don't know how you're ever going to top this."

"Well, one day when we're not in college, and we both have good jobs, we'll travel the world and see the sunset on every continent, on mountain tops, beaches, and anywhere else we can think of. This is just the beginning, baby."

I think I melted in my chair right then as I swooned. Oz Francisco was the most romantic man on the planet, and I knew I'd love him until my very last breath.

"Do you know what you're going to have?" He asked after a few minutes. "I see the waiter coming."

"I do," I answered as a tall, lanky guy about our age came up the path and stepped up by the table.

"Good evening, I'm Cesar, and I'll be your waiter for the

night. If you need anything, here's my number." He placed a card with a number written on it down on the table. "Since you can't wave me down, I thought this was best. Have you decided on what you'd like to eat tonight?"

"Thank you," I looked up from my menu. "I'm going to try the ahi tuna with mushroom risotto, and can I get a glass of sparkling water?"

"Of course, ma'am. And for you, sir?" he looked to Oz.

"I'm going to have the special."

"Good choices. I'll be back with your dinners as soon as they come up," Cesar smiled.

"And two chocolate soufflés," Oz said as the waiter started to walk away.

"Yes, sir."

I waited until he walked away before I stood up and straddled Oz's lap. "You're really going all out tonight, and I want to thank you."

His hands skated up the outside of my thighs and underneath the hem of my dress. "You can thank me all you want once it's dark."

I swung my legs around to sit sideways in his lap. I was going to make it difficult on Oz if he was adamant about waiting, which was so unlike him.

The sky started to change colors into these dark pink and oranges as our waiter brought our food out to us. He lit the candle in the center of our table before he left again. As he hit the shore, tiny twinkling lights all around us lit up and created a heart.

"Oz," I clutched my hands to my chest in awe of everything he'd done for tonight. "This is so sweet. I think I might cry."

With his arms around me, Oz rocked us from side to side. "If you need to cry, then cry."

I loved how understanding he was. Most guys hated it when women cried.

"I know," I squeezed his neck. "My therapist says it's very healthy to cry, but I don't want to ruin my makeup tonight. Plus, I want to eat this yummy food." Kissing his cheek once again, I slipped from his lap and into my chair.

Just as I was about to take the last bite of my risotto, two dolphins jumped out of the water. They were the perfect silhouette against the fading sun. "Did you orchestrate that too?"

Oz chuckled beside me. "I wish I was that good, but no. I did set this up, though." He stood as the waiter came with our dessert, placing them on the table, and then started to scatter rose petals all over the surrounding ground. The waiter walked backward, back down the path, still throwing the petals.

When I looked back at Oz, he was down on one knee, a box in hand, opened to the most beautiful ring I had ever seen. Taking my left hand in his trembling one, Oz beamed up at me.

"I know we're young. Too young to get married, in fact, but I know you're the one for me, and I believe I'm the one for you too. While I'm down on one knee before you asking if you'll spend the rest of your life with me, I don't want us to get married tomorrow, but once we've graduated and I can save up for the wedding you deserve. I'm so proud to call you my girlfriend. You're the strongest woman I know, and if it wasn't for you, I wouldn't be the man I am today. I vow to keep growing and becoming a better man for you, and I hope one day I'll be worthy of you."

Falling down on my knees, I took Oz's face between my hands and pressed kisses all over his face, punctuating each of my words. "You are already the man I deserve, and you always have been. Yes, you've made mistakes, but so have I. We all have, but that's life, and I can't wait to spend the rest of mine with you screwing up, loving you, and creating a family with you."

"Is that a yes, then?" He looked up at me with wide, happy eyes.

"It's more than a yes. I'd love nothing more." I pressed my mouth to his in the hottest, wettest, and most sultry kiss ever.

Oz stood up with me in his arms. Once my feet were firmly planted on the ground, he slipped the ring on my finger. "I didn't think this over as well as I thought I did. You can barely see the ring in this light."

"It doesn't matter what it looks like. I will love it no matter what. I know it's beautiful by the way it's sparkling in the fairy lights." I held my hand out, watching the light shimmer in the diamond. "Is this why you've been working so much this summer?"

"You deserve the best ring I could possibly buy, and I wanted to work for it and not buy it with the trust money."

Oz working for my engagement ring made it that much more special. "I love you so much." I squealed. "I can't believe we're engaged. Do you really want to wait until we graduate?"

"Yes, I want us to focus on school and to build our relationship even further, but I want you to know that I'm committed to my life with you." Leaning down, he kissed my forehead.

"You didn't have to buy me an engagement ring to show me that. I already know you're committed." Running my hands up his chest, my fingers started to undo the buttons of his shirt. "I think it's time to celebrate."

"I agree." His hands made their way under my dress and then swiftly removed my panties.

He lowered us down to the ground, my back hitting the hardwood. "Damn it," he cursed. "I should have brought a blanket for us." Oz immediately rectified the situation by moving to lie down with his back to the pier. He pulled his shirt off and placed it underneath him, and pulled me on top of him with my knees slightly cushioned by his shirt.

"I'm fine." While leaning down, I started to undo his pants. His stiff erection pressing against the zipper made it difficult to unzip him. I took another look around, astonished Oz had planned all of this without me knowing.

Slipping my hand inside his pants, I pulled his thick shaft out and relished in the silky steel and weight of him in my hand. "This is the best day of my life." I leaned down and nipped his bottom lip. "I love you."

"You should know by now I'll do anything for you. All you have to do is ask." He thrust up into my hand.

Placing both hands on his chest, I brushed my mouth to his as I started to rub my wet center along his cock before I took him in my hand and guided him to my entrance. Slowly I slid down, relishing in the feel of impaling myself and the accompanying stretch as I took him in. Oz's hands slid to my ass and held on tight. The feel of the rough pads of his fingers digging into my flesh spurred me on. I rocked and swiveled my hips as our mouths connected, our tongues moving in the same hurried state as our bodies.

When one of his hands moved to cup and then pinched my nipple, making a jolt of pleasure zipped through my body, I moved faster, slamming down on his length. Each time I bottomed out, my body started to tingle and fill with heat. My walls fluttered as I began to detonate. Oz's hands cupped my breasts and thrust his hips up as he came deep inside of me. The feel of his hot seed coating my insides took me over the edge with him.

Collapsing on top of Oz, I panted as I placed a kiss over his rapidly beating heart. As my world started to slow down, I listened to the waves crash against the shore. I tried to ingrain everything that had happened tonight in my brain. I never wanted to forget how special tonight was.

Oz's hands ran over my overheated skin, never stopping their movement.

A thought popped into my head that had me worried. I looked up at Oz. "Did Dani know about your plan?"

"She did, and she said she was perfectly fine with me asking you. It probably helps that she's in love."

"Probably, but I'm worried about her." I propped my chin on my hands and looked up at him. "How are they going to continue their relationship while Declan's in Spain playing soccer?"

"That I can't say, but when we saw him earlier this summer, he seemed like he wanted it to work."

"He looked at her the way you look at me," I kissed the dimple in his chin.

Some days it still amazed me we were an us, and Oz loved me, even if something horrific did have to happen for us to finally be together.

"Then they're golden if he feels for her anything like what I feel for you," he said, running his fingers through my hair.

Still, I would worry about Dani now that I didn't plan to go back to UCLA. "I wish she'd go to school here," I said as I laid my head back down on his chest.

"I do too, but we don't have the best women's soccer team here."

But we were here. Still, I understood Dani needed to do what was best for her if she was going to make it to the Olympics.

"What do you say we eat our dessert? Then we can take a walk along the beach and go home to celebrate."

"It does smell good, so I'd hate for it to go to waste." I moved to stand up and pulled my dress down to cover my ass. I didn't think anyone could see me, but I didn't want to take the chance.

We sat back down at the table. I took one bite of my soufflé, and I was in love. Even cold, it was the best damn dessert I'd ever had. Oz's eyes lit up as I moaned around my spoon. His blue eyes heated as he licked his lips, making me want to jump him again. We were never going to make it home if he kept being so irresistible.

Oz must have sensed my dilemma. He sat up and cleared his throat. "Did you really have no idea? I thought for sure you'd figure it out."

"If Fin wouldn't have said anything, I would have

assumed it was a regular date. Once he said something tonight, I thought maybe you were working to save money to finish the basement or part of it, so we'd have more privacy."

"Damn, why didn't I think of that? Maybe the guys and I can work on it. I wouldn't want to spend too much money since we'll only be here a couple more years, and it's not my place."

"It doesn't need to be anything fancy, but walls, a door, and electricity would be nice." Even as I said it, I realized it might be more than the guys could handle. I was sure they could put up the walls, but electricity was a whole other matter.

Oz nodded. "Two years is a long time to have everyone listening to us. Now that you've put the idea in my head, I want to give us some privacy. I think it would be best for all of us," he chuckled.

I took another bite and caught the light on my ring, and held it out, watching as it shimmered. "I think I'm going to be staring down at my ring for the foreseeable future. I can't believe we're engaged."

I was so happy my insides were bubbling up with excitement. I felt like I could explode at any moment. I was surprised I wasn't bouncing in my seat.

"Me neither, but seeing my ring on your finger has me wanting to pound my chest. You're mine," he growled, leaning over and sucked my bottom lip into his mouth.

"And you're mine. Maybe I should get a ring for you to wear and stake my claim."

"You've got nothing to worry about. I'll forever be yours, ring or not." He stood and knelt down, taking off my heels before he held out his hand for me to take. We walked hand in hand down to the water and then along the shore as the tide washed over our feet and slipped away over and over again.

I couldn't take my eyes off Oz. My fiancé and future husband, and he couldn't take his eyes off me.

Everything I went through almost a year ago was worth finally having this moment. When I was at my darkest and lowest of lows, I never thought my nightmare would end with Oz. If he hadn't taken me in, I didn't know where I'd be. Maybe I'd still be locked in my dorm room, or possibly something much worse. Instead, I was in love with the man of my dreams, and I couldn't wait to spend the rest of my life with him and see where our journey took us. I knew no matter what happened, good or bad, Oz would be by my side. This was just our beginning. Our first down.

WANT MORE of Fin and West? Read AWAY GAME today. Ford's story is coming May 13, 2022 in OVER TIME.

Did you enjoy FIRST DOWN? If so, please consider leaving a review on Goodreads, Amazon, or BookBub. Reviews mean the world to authors especially to authors who are starting out. You can help get your favorite books into the hands of new readers.

I'd appreciate your help in spreading the word and it will only take a moment to leave a quick review. It can be as short or as long as you like. Your review could be the deciding factor or whether or not someone else buys my book.

To stay up to date on all my releases subscribe to my newsletter. https://ellakade.com/newsletter/

ACKNOWLEDGMENTS

My family- your support means so much. Thank you for all of your encouragement and giving me the time to do what makes me happy.

Kelsey: If it wasn't for our online writing, I'm not sure how many books I'd get done. Thank you for always being there.

To my **girls**: QB Tyler , Carmel Rhodes, Erica Marselas. I love each and every one of you. Thank you for all of your support.

Thank you **Kristen Breanne** for making my story into a book.

To all my **author friends**, you know who you are. Thank you for accepting me and making me feel welcome in this amazing community.

To **Wildfire Marketing Solutions and Shauna**, thank you for all your knowledge and for helping me make Away Game a success!

Lovers thank you for always being there.

Team Harlow's Girls: Each and everyone of you are amazing. Thank you for all of your support. You ROCK!

To each and every **reader**, **reviewer**, and **blogger** - I would be nowhere without you. Thank you for taking a chance on an unknown author.

ABOUT ELLA

Ella Kade is a forbidden and dark romance writer who enjoys writing captivating characters with sinful intent.

Read Ella to get immersed into her words where she ruins lives and slowly puts them back together.

ALSO BY ELLA KADE